girls just wanna have pugs

Also by J.J. Howard

The Love Pug

Pugs in a Blanket

Pugs and Kisses

Sit, Stay, Love

girls just wanna have pugs

j.j. howard

SCHOLASTIC INC.

ISBN 978-1-338-64042-7

10 9 8 7 6 5 4 3 2 1   21 22 23 24 25

Printed in the U.S.A.   40
First printing 2021

Book design by Yaffa Jaskoll

This one's for my girls—aka the Chicas—Nikki, Beth, and Carol. Love you guys.

1

Missing Meatball

Early Friday morning, I was in my apartment, getting ready for school, when I heard my neighbor's voice in the hallway.

"Meatballllllll!" she was calling.

My neighbors Sarah and Dan Thompson had the cutest dog in our entire building: a small—and very round—black pug named Meatball. And Sarah's calling for him loudly could only mean one thing: Meatball had gotten out and was on the loose.

After I finished lacing up my sneakers, I opened the door to peek out into the hall. "Sarah? What's going on?" I asked.

"Oh, Kat!" Sarah said when she saw me. "Maybe you could

help? I was getting the twins dressed and Dan Jr. must have opened the door . . . Anyway, Meatball ran out and now I can't find him!"

I had to remind myself not to roll my eyes at the mention of Dan Jr. Sarah and Dan were very nice people, but if you asked me, their oldest child was an absolute terror. I even caught him pulling poor little Meatball's tail once. Sarah and her husband always seemed frazzled, and I sometimes helped them out by walking Meatball. I never minded; Meatball was the best.

"I'm worried he ran to the stairs," Sarah said. She pointed down the hall to the door that led to the stairwell; our maintenance person had left the door propped open. "What if he goes down to the lobby and runs outside?"

"I'm sure he won't do that," I told her. "After all, it's four floors down. And Marcel wouldn't let him out," I added, thinking of our kindhearted doorman. "I'll help you look," I offered. "You go down and I'll go up. Okay?"

"Great! But . . . I don't want to make you late for school . . ."

"It's still really early," I said, stepping outside the apartment. "Besides, I want to find Meatball, too."

I liked to wake up early so I didn't have to rush getting ready for school. Meanwhile, my little sister, Micki, was probably still sleeping in her room. I was always antsy waiting for her in the mornings. Our mom had already left for work (she's an early bird, too), and our dad was, as usual, away on a business trip.

"Okay, do you have your phone?" Sarah asked. I nodded, patting my jeans pocket. "I can text you if I find him—and vice versa."

"Got it," I said, and headed for the stairwell.

I climbed up to the sixth floor and called for Meatball. But there was no sign of him anywhere. I pulled out my phone. No text from Sarah.

It seemed unlikely to me that Meatball would go too far up or down. He wasn't that fond of stairs, or any sort of exercise, really. He must have gotten himself turned around and now he was probably scared and hiding in a corner somewhere. Our building, the Burgundy, was big and old, with lots of little nooks and crannies.

Then an idea hit me: What Meatball *did* love was food. Whenever I walked him, he always perked up if I had a treat with me. And I knew that his absolute favorite food was hot dogs. If Meatball was hiding and he smelled hot dogs, he would definitely come running.

I ran back downstairs and into my apartment. I found some hot dogs in the freezer, quickly microwaved two of them, and then cut them up and shoved them in a ziplock baggie.

As soon as I stepped back into the hallway with the hot dogs, I heard the telltale snuffling sound of a hungry Meatball. The little pug emerged from the nook he'd been hiding in at the west end of the hall and came barreling toward me on his short little legs.

"Hey, boy," I told him, petting his back and giving him small bites of hot dog.

I wiped my hands on my pants—whoops, forgot to grab a paper towel or a napkin—and texted Sarah.

I gave Meatball a few more bites of his unearned treat and then sat down on the floor beside him. He curled against my legs, looking up at me adoringly. Well, he knew I had another whole hot dog in a baggie, so maybe that explained *some* of his adoration. But his fur was so soft, and his little face was so darn cute—I couldn't help but give him a thorough petting while we waited.

When Sarah reached us, she was crying a little in relief. "Kat, thank you. I just don't know what I would have done without your quick thinking."

I felt a warm glow knowing I'd been able to help. "Anything for Meatball," I said, giving the pug one last pat before Sarah scooped him up and brought him back into her apartment.

I went into my apartment and put the leftover hot dog bites in the fridge. I was washing my hands when Micki appeared in the kitchen, fully dressed, thankfully. Micki and I look almost exactly alike: We both have medium-brown, shoulder-length, straight hair; pale skin; and hazel eyes. We're only three years apart, but I'd always felt much more grown-up.

"What were you doing?" Micki asked, yawning. "I heard you coming in and out the door."

"I had to help Sarah find Meatball," I explained. "He got loose."

"Did he drool on you?" Micki asked, pulling a Pop-Tart out of the cabinet. Micki didn't like dogs as much as I did.

"No, he did not!" I said. "Anyway, can you grab me a Pop-Tart, too, please? And not one of the blueberry ones."

Micki made a sheepish face and put back the one she'd grabbed before handing me one of her favorites, a Frosted Brown Sugar Cinnamon. I love my little sister, but she will fully hoard the best snacks if she thinks she can get away with it.

As I went to toast my Pop-Tart, I noticed the folded note Mom had left propped up against the toaster for me. I sighed as I scooped up the note and put it in my backpack. I had a feeling I knew what it said.

"What's that?" Micki asked as she wolfed down her Pop-Tart (she likes hers untoasted).

"Don't worry about it," I told her. I pulled my freshly toasted breakfast out of the toaster and took a big bite. "We should get going."

We grabbed our backpacks and headed out into the hallway. I texted my best friends, Lucy and Taz, who also live in our building, to ask if they wanted to walk to school with us. Lucy wrote back that she'd gone in early for something with Drama Club. Taz didn't text back, but that was pretty typical Taz. She'd see the text sometime later, after it didn't matter anymore.

Micki and I walked downstairs, since waiting for the elevator in the Burgundy usually takes longer. We said good morning to Marcel in the lobby, and then stepped out into the broiling heat of the September day in New York City. School had started last week, but it still felt like summer. Our school was only a few blocks away, but when it was super hot, the walk seemed longer. I couldn't wait for the crisp fall weather—my favorite—to finally get here. The brick buildings and stone town houses of my Upper West Side neighborhood always looked especially pretty with orange and red leaves tumbling to the sidewalk.

The note in my backpack was bothering me. By the time Micki and I got to school and went to our separate homerooms, I had decided to just read it and get it over with.

I took my usual seat in Mrs. Jackson's room and flipped open the note from Mom:

Dear Kat,
I talked to your father yesterday and we are both concerned about the fact that you have not signed up

for an extracurricular activity again this year. We are proud of your grades, but as we've discussed, grades aren't enough. It's time to get started now building that resumé, for high school and eventually college! I got a list from your homeroom teacher of all the activities you can sign up for this year. So be thinking which one—or more!—you want to pick _before_ we talk to Dad on Skype tonight.

Love,

Mom

I groaned. My parents were so predictable; they brought this same issue up with me at the start of every school year. And Mom always wrote me a note, instead of sending a text or bringing it up in person, because she thought it seemed more "serious" that way.

As Mrs. Jackson began to read the weekly lunch menu in a monotone voice, I thought about what I could sign up for as a school activity. Lucy was in drama, but I knew that wasn't for me. I'd practically had a heart attack that time I had to read a poem in front of the whole school last year. And Taz was in the Art Club and the Fashion Club. But I was pretty much hopeless at both art *and* fashion. I looked down at my plain blue T-shirt and jeans. Yep, boring.

What *did* I like? Well, I liked being organized, for one. I liked being prepared and getting good grades. But that was all curricular—not *extra*. I felt defeated. Since when wasn't it enough to be neat, organized, prepared, and always on time?

I drummed my fingers on my desk, and then remembered something else I liked—no, *loved*. Dogs! I'd even written up a sales pitch to present to my parents about why I should have my own dog. But I knew I had to be strategic and wait to discuss that topic with them when they were both in good moods.

The bell rang to signal the end of homeroom, and I went out to my locker, where Lucy was waiting for me.

"Hey, Kat!" She took one look at me and her face fell. "Oh . . . *hey*—what's the matter?"

Lucy's been my best friend since fourth grade, so she knows me really well.

"It's just this," I said, handing her the note from my mom.

She read it, nodding. "You knew your parents were going to bug you about this again."

"Yeah, but it still . . . I don't know, stings?" I pulled out my books for the morning and slammed my locker shut. "I can't exactly help that I'm not good at sports, or theater, *or* art."

"There are lots of other extracurriculars. You're being too hard on yourself," Lucy said.

"Again?" Taz asked, coming up to her locker, which was one down from mine.

"What do you mean, 'again'?" I asked with an indignant sniff.

"I mean 'again' as in another time. You're always being too hard on yourself, Cabot."

"According to my parents, I'm not being hard *enough* on myself," I grumbled, leaning back against the lockers and showing Taz the note from Mom.

"Luce is right," Taz said. "There are tons of activities. Just pick one."

"Easy for you to say. I want to pick something I'm halfway interested in. Also hopefully, you know, sort of good at."

It was Taz's turn to shove her locker door shut. "Or preferably the best at."

"Hey!" I frowned. But I also knew Taz was kind of right. Maybe that was why I'd been putting off picking an activity for so long. I didn't want to fail. It was why I'd never join the drama or art or fashion clubs, as much as I loved hanging with my two BFFs.

"Taz!" Lucy said.

"Kat knows I've got her number," Taz said with her usual Taz-level confidence.

Taz and Lucy are both really confident, actually. Taz has long, shiny, dark-brown hair; brown skin; and big brown eyes. She always finds the most interesting clothes and jewelry in vintage stores. Once I went with her to some thrift stores and decided to get something interesting, too. That led to the Vest Incident of 2018, which is something I don't like to talk or even think about, so that was pretty much the end of my fashion bravery. Lucy is really tall, and she has blond hair and blue eyes and looks sort of like an old-fashioned doll who came to life. Beside both of them, I think I look pretty boring.

The bell rang for first period. I headed down the hall with my friends, feeling jealous that they both had that certain something extra they were good at. I had no idea what that was for me. But I would have a super-fun Skype meeting about it tonight.

2

Welcome to the Burgundy, Declan Ward

I noticed the dog first.

I was heading home from school alone. Mom had picked up Micki early to take her to the dentist, and my two busy friends were staying after school to create art and theater.

Then, across the street, I spotted the second-cutest pug I'd ever seen, after Meatball: a tiny white puppy with a super-wrinkly forehead. The pug was being walked by a boy who looked to be about my age. Both the boy and the dog turned onto 86th Street. My street. Wait. They were headed right for the Burgundy!

I picked up my pace and managed to reach the entrance of the Burgundy just as Marcel was opening up the door for the boy and the adorable puppy.

The boy thanked Marcel, and I did, too, as I hurried into the building.

"I like your dog," I said to the boy, a little out of breath.

The boy turned around and said, "Thanks!" Up close, I could see that he was ridiculously cute, with dark wavy hair, pale skin, and bright green eyes. I'd never seen a person, maybe not even on TV, with eyes that green.

"Good afternoon, Kat," Marcel said, giving me a smile and leaning over to pat the pug's head. "Kat loves dogs," Marcel explained to the boy.

"That's true," I said.

"So do I," said the boy, grinning at me. "Hi, Kat. I'm Declan Ward."

"Um, hi, Declan," I said, trying not to blush. "Do you live in the building?"

Declan nodded as we walked farther into the lobby. The puppy hurried forward, pulling on the leash. "My dad and I just moved in this morning."

"Oh, well, welcome to the Burgundy!"

"Thank you, young lady," a voice said. I whirled around and saw that an older version of Declan had stepped out of the mail room.

"This is my dad," Declan said. "He likes to interrupt people."

"Just being friendly, lad." Declan's dad had an Irish accent, I noticed, but his son didn't. I decided it was probably a good thing, because being that cute plus having an accent would be completely and *utterly* ridiculous. I also filed away the fact that his dad was also one of those "young lady" dads, which seemed less annoying with the accent for some reason.

"Your dog is sooo cute," I told Declan as the three of us—plus the puppy—headed toward the elevator. "How old is he—or she?"

"She's ten weeks old," Declan said. "We just adopted her. She's my guilt puppy. Dad said we could get her when he told me we were moving."

"Indeed I did," Declan's dad said. We stopped in front of the elevator, and he pressed the button to call it down to the lobby. "We moved here from Dublin, Ireland," Mr. Ward added. "But we were in Los Angeles before that. That's where Declan grew up."

That explained Declan's lack of an accent.

"I'm sure moving is hard, but it's almost worth it to have a puppy of your own," I said. "My parents say we're not allowed to have a dog. Can I pet her?"

"Sure. She's quite friendly," Declan's dad said.

I knelt down and petted two of the softest ears in all of puppy-dom. "What's her name?" I asked Declan.

"We call her Sparky. Her actual name is Spark Pug. It's, like, a play on words . . ."

"I get it! Instead of Spark *Plug*. Clever." I leaned in closer and Sparky started licking my face. I giggled.

"I'm sorry your parents say you can't have a dog," Declan said. The elevator arrived and we all went inside, Sparky leading the way. "You're obviously good with them."

Again, I tried my best not to blush. "Thanks," I said, pressing the button for the fifth floor. Declan pressed the button for the fourth. "Are you going to school in the neighborhood?" I asked Declan as the elevator slowly rose up. "I go to M.S. 243."

"Is that the one on 84th Street? If so, I'm enrolling on Monday."

"Yes, sure is," I said with a nod. I tried not to smile too widely after learning that the cute new boy would be going to my school. "What grade are you in?"

"I'm in eighth," he said.

"Me too!" I replied.

"You know, we're going to have to figure out a plan for who will take Sparky on her walks if you ever have to stay late after school," Mr. Ward said to Declan. "I sometimes have to travel for work," he explained to me.

"So does my dad," I replied. I was about to say that *I'd* be happy to walk Sparky sometimes, but then the elevator dinged and the door opened onto the fourth floor.

"This is us," Declan said. "See you around the building—or

at school!" he said, and he, Sparky, and Mr. Ward stepped off the elevator.

I waved, feeling my heart give a little flutter as the elevator door closed. I thought about the possibility of walking Sparky. That would be so fun. The elevator got to my floor, and I walked toward my apartment, rummaging in my backpack for my key. I started thinking about the Skype call and my parents bugging me to find an activity and BOOM—I had an idea.

I could start a dog-walking business!

I'd been trying so hard to think of one thing I liked. But this idea combined *two* things I liked: dogs and being organized. I'd never run any type of business before, but you definitely had to be organized to be successful. I knew that from my dad, who worked in business. I also knew that to start a business, you had to have customers. Which was perfect, because there were loads of dogs right here in the Burgundy, with busy owners who worked full-time, or older owners who could use the extra help, especially on days when the elevator was out. Carrying a dog up and down the stairs wasn't so easy for an older person.

Maybe I could even get my friends on board, so we could walk more dogs at different times.

As I entered my apartment, I felt a new bounce in my step. I finally had an idea to share with my parents. I could only hope they—and my friends—would agree to it.

3

Remote Control

I hung up my backpack in its usual spot and sent a text to Lucy, asking her to stop by when she was done with Drama Club. Since she lived on the seventh floor of the Burgundy, my apartment was technically on her way home. She texted back right away:

Leaving school now. See you soon!

I paced around the apartment, waiting for her. As soon as Lucy knocked on the door, I practically dragged her inside.

"What's going on?" she asked.

"You know how I was trying to think of an activity to get involved in?" I began, and Lucy nodded. "Well, I had an idea!"

"Great. Which club are you going to join?" Lucy asked as we headed for the kitchen. "I'm getting some juice—you want some?"

Lucy and I were the kind of friends who no longer asked permission to get stuff at each other's places. And we both knew where everything was.

"No, thanks, I'm okay. But listen, it's not a *club* I want to join. I want to start a business."

"A business?" Lucy said, setting down her backpack on the kitchen floor. "Hmm. What kind of business? Don't you need money to start one?"

I hopped up to sit on a stool. "Not if it's a service we'd be providing. And we wouldn't have any expenses," I explained. "I'm going to start a dog-walking business—here in the Burgundy! And . . . I'm hoping you'll be a part of it."

Lucy opened the refrigerator and took out a carton of orange juice. "So you're going to walk dogs for people who live in the building and charge them for it?" She still sounded skeptical—Lucy always had a lot of questions. But luckily, I had answers.

"Yep," I said. "I mean, *we* would walk the dogs. I'm going to ask Taz, too. I figure we'll have set rates, depending on how far we take the dogs. Some people probably just want their dogs taken to the closest patch of grass to make their business. But we could also take the dogs all the way to the dog run in Riverside Park. And that could cost more. I would organize everything—you know how much I love organizing things."

"Oh, I definitely know *that*," Lucy said, smiling. She poured herself a tall glass of orange juice, then added, "So, it would be like Uber, for dog walking?"

"Exactly!" I said, beaming. "I'm actually thinking that Taz could help design an app so clients could get in touch with us that way." I paused. "What do you think?"

Lucy took a sip of juice, then grinned. "I like it. I don't know how much time I'll have until after the play is over. *But* I'm trying to save up for this acting seminar over winter break. So . . . I'm in!"

I felt a burst of relief. "Yay! I was hoping you'd say that!" I jumped off the stool and gave Lucy a big hug.

"But, Kat, I've never walked a dog before. You'll have to show me the ropes."

I giggled. "That's almost a pun. The ropes. Like leashes?"

Lucy made a wry face. "A bit of a stretch, but okay. So you'll show me, then?"

"Sure! I've walked Meatball loads of times. It's super easy. But listen—you also have to help me come up with the perfect name for the business. You're good at that creative stuff."

Lucy nodded. "I'll start brainstorming."

"Great, thank you. I'm telling my parents about the idea tonight, since we're having our Skype 'family meeting.'"

Lucy's face fell a bit. "Kat, I hate to break it to you when you're so excited, but I think your parents want you to sign up for a *school* activity."

It was my face's turn to fall. "Ugh. You're probably right. But there's definitely no dog-walking club—or business—at school."

"No . . . but there *is* some kind of a business club. I remember from when Ms. Kennedy was reading us the activities list in homeroom the other day . . ." Lucy bent down, unzipped her backpack, and pulled out her phone. "I'm pretty sure the list is posted on the school website."

She scrolled for a few seconds and then said, "Aha! Here's

the list. Archery, art, chess, cooking, drama, fashion, gaming, ooh—here it is! Junior FBLA."

"What's an FBLA?" I asked, leaning over to look at the screen.

"Future Business Leaders of America," Lucy explained. "And it's a new club this year—see, it's marked with an asterisk? Which means they haven't even had club meetings yet."

"Lucy, you're a genius!" I said, hugging her again and squishing her phone between us.

"Thanks," Lucy said, laughing.

"Who's the advisor?" I asked.

"I think it's Ms. Weinstein. She seems nice. Taz had her last year for math."

"Well, as long as it isn't Mrs. Jackson," I said, thinking of my strict homeroom teacher. "Anyway, this FBLA is the answer to my prayers—a school club to make my parents happy, *and* I still get to launch my business idea. Thank goodness you came by, Luce!"

"Here to help. But I have to go—Mom asked me to put something in the oven for dinner."

"Okay. But hey—don't tell Taz yet, okay? I want to tell her myself. I'll invite you guys over tomorrow to discuss everything."

"Sounds good. Later, Kitty-Kat!"

Lucy grabbed her bag and headed for the door. I sat back down on the stool with a happy sigh. Now I felt ready to face tonight's family meeting.

Our apartment door opened and Micki burst in, followed by Mom.

"I got a tooth pulled. See?" Micki's mouth came much too close to my eyeballs.

"Eww, Mom, make her stop!"

"Micki," Mom said in a warning tone, but it was halfhearted.

My parents treated me like I had to be perfect, but Micki always seemed to get a pass.

"Why did you have to get your tooth pulled?" I asked Micki.

"She's being dramatic. It was her last baby tooth and it was loose," Mom said.

I rolled my eyes. Typical Micki making something sound much more exciting than it actually was.

"It still counts," Micki responded.

A gift for you

Happy birthday, Remy! From Sydney

 amazon Gift Receipt

Send a Thank You Note

You can learn more about your gift or start a return here too.

Scan using the Amazon app or visit
https://a.co/cP8N9ia

Pax

Order ID: 114-0347792-7433853   Ordered on April 25, 2021

"So, I see you got my note this morning?" Mom asked me, nodding toward the toaster.

"Yep," I said, smiling. "And I have an activity all picked out, thank you very much."

Mom looked surprised. "You do? What is it?"

"You'll find out at our family meeting," I told her, crossing my arms over my chest.

Now Mom rolled her eyes. "Okay, Miss Katherine. Listen, help me set the table."

"Can't we just eat in front of the TV since Dad's not here?" Micki asked in a whine.

Mom wavered and then gave in. "Okay, fine. But only because we're just having leftover spaghetti. Next time I actually cook, we're setting the table."

Micki offered me her palm for a low five and I slapped it. Mom shook her head and went to her bedroom to change. Dinner in front of the TV for Mom meant yoga pants and an old T-shirt. I decided that sounded like a good idea, too, and went to my own room to change into comfy clothes.

*   *   *

A couple of hours later, Mom hooked up her laptop to our living room TV, and the Skype call from Dad came through. He was sitting in some hotel room, with his laptop in front of him. He looked the same as the last time we'd seen him in person about a month ago, but extra tired.

After we all waved and said hello, Mom announced that I'd chosen an extracurricular activity. She turned expectantly to me.

"I'm joining Junior FBLA," I announced. "And I'm starting my own dog-walking business here in the Burgundy."

Dad seemed to think about it for a few seconds. "I like the sound of FBLA. I was in the same club when I was in high school, and it's a great organization. The dog-walking thing could be a good way to practice the skills you learn in the club, just as long as it doesn't interfere with your studies."

I nodded, feeling kind of let down. I didn't know what I'd been expecting from Dad. Excitement, maybe? But before I knew it, he was moving on to the next topic. And it soon became clear that he was determined to do a month's worth of parenting in one Skype call. First, he asked me to get my school schedule and read it off to him, and then he asked me—and Mom—why I wasn't taking Mandarin as my world language class, since it was now being offered at our school. He said he remembered reading that in the parent newsletter.

"They are offering it," Mom said. "But Kat's been taking Spanish since sixth grade. And she did really well on the placement test—she's going to get high school credit for this year's class."

"Yeah, I love Spanish," I chimed in. "My teacher says if I keep working at this pace I'll be ahead by college." My heart started beating fast. Would Dad *really* make me switch language classes?

Dad looked at me over the top of his glasses. "Kat, it's not really about what class or teacher you like the most. It's about what will serve you best going forward. And I can tell you right now that learning Mandarin will give you a leg up in business."

I didn't say anything. Yes, maybe I wanted to follow in Dad's footsteps and go into business—I'd just told him that with my choice of activity. But I didn't even know how much I'd like FBLA yet. And if I did, I had a long time to get ready for my eventual business career.

I turned to Mom. She knew how much I was looking forward to Spanish class this year. I watched her mouth set into the determined line that only appeared when she was about to *not* give in. Whew.

Before Mom got the chance to say anything, though, Dad asked to hear Micki's schedule. He stopped Mom when she got to her math class. "You didn't say *honors*—Micki needs to be in the highest-level math class."

"It didn't fit with the elective she chose," Mom said.

"What elective? That space exploration thing you mentioned? That doesn't sound useful."

"She's very excited about it," Mom said.

Micki had been distracted, playing with the tassels on one of the sofa's throw pillows, until she heard Dad mention her space elective. "Wait, what? Dad, I *have* to take that class. Mr. Sarles already asked me to be his assistant and everything, since I had the highest grade in science last year—remember how I won the award?"

Dad frowned. "You're in sixth grade, Micki. I don't think

you need to be worrying about helping out a teacher. You can take it next year, if it fits . . ."

But he didn't say anymore, since Micki had burst into tears. Mom glared at Dad and then went over to Micki. My little sister wrapped her arms around Mom and kept sobbing, and Mom led Micki back to her room.

Then it was just me sitting there awkwardly with Dad. "So, how's Barcelona?" I asked him.

"I'm in Madrid."

"Oh." It seemed sort of ironic that he was in Spain after the argument we'd just had about Spanish, but luckily Mom came back in just then.

"Say good-night to your dad, Kat," she said in her don't-even-ask-a-single-question voice. So I did as she said and then went back to my room.

I heard Mom's voice rise as she talked to Dad, but she must have turned down the volume on him because I only heard her. When she came to check on me later her neck was pink and splotchy, like it gets when she's really upset.

"I'm sorry, Kat," she said. "Please don't worry. You're taking Spanish this year." Her face had that determined look again.

"And Micki's space elective?"

She nodded. "Yes. She's taking it."

"Thanks, Mom." I went over and put my arms around her, and she hugged me back.

"Of course. But don't be too hard on your dad. It's difficult for him to be gone so much."

I didn't really see how Dad trying to control everything from so far away was difficult for *him*. But I didn't want Mom to turn any pinker, so I just hugged her again and said good-night.

4

Paws for Effect

"Micki!" I said, opening my bedroom door after my sister had knocked for the fifth time. "Can you go back to your room, please?"

Usually Micki can watch all the *Descendants* movies on a continuous loop. But even though she'd just started watching the second movie in her room, she'd come out and decided to interrupt the first-ever meeting of my new business.

"Can't we make cookies instead?" Micki pleaded, peeking past me into my room, where Lucy and Taz were lounging on my two beanbag chairs. "Come on, Kat! It's Saturday!"

I took a deep breath. Normally I would have asked Mom for help, but she'd had to go into her office last minute.

"Not right now, okay?" I told Micki. "If you go back and watch your movie, we'll make cookies afterward. Deal?"

I watched Micki consider my offer. She wasn't usually into delayed gratification, but after a few seconds she nodded, then left my doorway and went back to her own room.

As I shut the door and turned back to my friends, I realized that Micki had actually been onto something. I *should* have prepared snacks for Lucy and Taz, since this was a pitch meeting. Lucy had already said yes, but that was a gimme. It was Taz who I needed to get on board.

"I wouldn't say no to cookies," Taz said, proving my point.

"We'll all make cookies," I promised my friends as I sat down on my bed. "But first . . . I'm super excited to tell you my idea. Are you ready?"

"Yes," Taz said, sitting up straighter. "I've been wondering what this mystery meeting is about. You're not moving away or something?"

"Gosh, no! Why would I be *excited* to tell you that?"

Lucy and I were both making horrified faces. The thought of moving away from New York, the greatest city in the world, was too horrible to even contemplate.

"Well, good. Then what's going on?" Taz asked.

"Okay, so you know how I was looking for an activity?"

Taz nodded. "You signed up for Junior FBLA. You texted me that yesterday."

"Yes, but . . . I also had an amazing idea for a business of my own. Well, *our* own. A dog-walking business, right here at the Burgundy!"

Taz's face lit up. "Cool! You mean we could earn money walking dogs?"

"Yep," I said, thrilled that Taz seemed into the idea. Lucy was grinning, too.

"This is perfect," Taz said. "I've been trying to save all my birthday money and allowance and everything for the past year, but I'm still way short."

"What are you saving for?" Lucy asked her.

"A Wacom Cintiq."

Lucy gave her a look. "Oh, that clears it up. So glad I asked."

"It's a tablet, one that's great for artists," Taz explained. "But it costs more than six hundred dollars, and I'm not even halfway there." She turned back to me. "Plus, we used to have a dog when I was little, before we moved to New York. Animals love me. So count me in."

"Awesome!" I said. I opened up the fresh notebook I'd prepared for the meeting and ran a line through the first item on the to-do list: Ask Taz to join. "Next up," I continued, "we have to choose a name. Luce, do you have an idea?"

"I do!" Lucy said, also sitting up straighter and beaming.

"Great," I said.

When Lucy didn't say anything else, I prompted, "Well, what is it?"

Lucy let out a sigh. "Jeez, I was trying to pause for dramatic effect. But fine. Get this: West Side Dog-Walking Story!"

Both Taz and I did pause then, but not for dramatic effect.

"Um . . ." I began, and felt a wave of relief when Taz took over.

"I just think it's kind of long . . ."

"But it's a play on the name of the musical!" Lucy protested. "*West Side Story*. And we live on the *West Side*. Get it?"

"We get it," Taz said, exchanging a glance with me. "And it's very clever. But what about something a little, you know, simpler?"

Lucy looked disappointed, but then said, "I had one other idea. It doesn't really make sense since there are only three of us. But what about Four Paws Dog Walking? Get it, like a play on *for* and *four*?"

She glanced anxiously from Taz to me.

Taz and I both broke into smiles.

"I like it!" I cried, and Taz nodded.

"It has a nice ring to it," Taz said.

"But again, there are only three of us . . ." Lucy pointed out.

"Three Paws doesn't sound as good," I said. "And, besides, maybe we'll add another dog walker if our business grows!"

Feeling satisfied, I wrote down:

Four Paws Dog-Walking Agency

"Great," Taz said. "Can we make cookies now?"

"Hang on," I said. "I had another agenda item. I think we should each have a specific role in the business—besides dog walker, of course. You know, like president, treasurer . . ."

"You should be the president, of course," Lucy said, and I blushed, feeling grateful since I'd been thinking that anyway.

"Yes, President Kat!" Taz cheered.

"Thanks, guys," I said. "I'll try to live up to the role." I glanced at Lucy. "Do you think you could be the treasurer?" I asked. "You're the best at math."

"Sure," Lucy said. "I can keep track of what we'll charge for each service and what we earn."

"How about me?" Taz asked.

"Well, I was going to ask if you could be in charge of design and technology," I began. "I wondered if you could even create an app for the business," I added, crossing my fingers.

To my relief, Taz beamed. "That sounds really cool," she said. "I'd love to do it."

"Perfect!" I said. I quickly wrote down our new roles in my notebook.

Katherine Cabot—President (and Founder)

Lucy Larrabee—Treasurer

Mumtaz "Taz" Topolsky—Director of Design
and Technology

Then I jumped off my bed and gave each of my friends a
high five. "Four Paws Dog-Walking Agency is up and running!"
I declared.

"Now . . . cookie time!" Taz added, and the three of us
cracked up.

"Okay, okay," I said, and led the way out of my room. Micki
was still holed up in hers watching the movie, but I knew she'd
emerge as soon as she heard the sounds of baking from the
kitchen.

I got out the cookie mix and Taz found the baking sheet while
Lucy took out the measuring cups. I measured everything carefully, making sure to clean up as I went along. Mom hates germs
and messes. If she came home and the kitchen wasn't clean—
even in the middle of cookie making—she would not be happy.

As predicted, Micki rushed eagerly into the kitchen just as I
was putting on my oven mitts.

"Yay, cookies!" she cried.

She watched as I carefully opened the oven door and even more carefully slid the baking sheet inside. It was only recently that Mom had decided to let us bake cookies without her supervision, and that was only after, like, one hundred practice sessions and lectures about oven safety. Micki still wasn't allowed near the oven unless I was there.

"I had a thought," Lucy said as I set the timer. "Before Four Paws can get up and running, how are people in the Burgundy going to find out we exist?"

"Right," I said, snapping my fingers. I knew I'd forgotten something. "I was thinking we could put up flyers in the laundry rooms announcing the new business." The Burgundy had a small laundry room on each floor.

"A flyer would be awesome," Lucy said. She and I both looked expectantly at Taz.

"Of *course* I can make the flyer!" Taz said, throwing her hands up. "I'll even design a logo, if you want."

"Thank you, Director of Design and Technology!" I said, giving Taz a hug.

"What are you guys talking about?" Micki asked.

"We're starting a business," Lucy told her.

"Can I be in it?"

"Maybe when you're a little bit older," I said.

"Ugh, that's literally always the answer to *everything*," Micki complained.

"Sorry," I said. I knew our parents wouldn't let Micki join in the dog-walking business yet. Besides, she didn't even like dogs that much.

The timer dinged and I pulled the cookies out of the oven. They looked perfect. But that wasn't a surprise; I'd followed the recipe perfectly. When Lucy made cookies she often added extra things to them, which sometimes tasted good, but also sometimes messed things up. I'd eaten more than one partially raw experimental cookie at my best friend's house. I guess how you make cookies probably says a lot about you as a person.

Using Mom's favorite spatula, I carefully transferred the cookies to a plate and let them cool, and then everybody dug in. Micki scarfed down two cookies in practically one bite, then returned to her room to finish the movie.

I looked happily at my friends, who were still savoring their treats. The cookies were a well-deserved reward for our first successful Four Paws meeting. I couldn't wait to start walking those doggos!

I remembered one more thing I needed to bring up with Lucy. "We need to do your training," I told her. "So I can show you the ropes?"

"Oh, yeah," Lucy said, her mouth full of cookie. "I have zero experience with dog walking," she explained to Taz.

"What if we asked Sarah if we could take Meatball out tomorrow?" I said to Lucy. "Get you started in the biz?"

"Sure," Lucy said. "Just text me."

"I can't be there," Taz said. "I have a Fashion Club meeting tomorrow and, you know, I also have a flyer to design," she added mischievously.

"That's no problem," I said. "With my help, Lucy will be an expert dog walker in no time."

5

Rule Number Two

"Wait, you want me to do *what*? With *that*?"

Lucy stared down at the grass in horror. I tried to stifle a giggle.

Sarah Thompson had been more than happy to loan us Meatball for a long walk on Sunday afternoon. As soon as we'd stepped out of the Burgundy, I'd handed Meatball's leash over to Lucy, who took it gingerly. I showed Lucy how to hold the leash a little more firmly and guide Meatball along. Everything had been going well, until we reached a patch of grass where Meatball had stopped to do his business. Now Meatball was done, but Lucy was frozen in fear, holding Meatball's leash in one hand while I tried to hand her a little plastic bag.

"Luce, you know you have to pick up the doggie poop as part of the job," I explained. "It's kind of rule number one. It's also literally the law."

"But he's not *my* dog . . . I mean it's just *sooo* gross."

Meatball barked up at Lucy, as if to say, *Who's gross? Not me!*

This time a giggle did escape me. "Yeah, but the owner's not here," I pointed out to Lucy. "You're filling in. That's the whole point. It's not like we can just plant a flag, and Sarah or Dan can come by to scoop the poop later."

Lucy's eyes flew up to meet mine. "That sounds like a great idea!"

I laughed, and then Lucy was laughing, too. "I know I'm being ridiculous. I've just never had to . . . touch dog poop before," she said. "Sorry, Meatball," she added.

Meatball barked again, sounding a little less huffy this time.

It wasn't that Lucy didn't like dogs; she just didn't have any experience with them. And in general, Lucy wasn't really used to cleaning up anything. Lucy's mom never made her do any sort of real chores. So I knew all of this was kind of a big step for Lucy.

"I understand," I told her. "And you don't actually have to touch it. See, the bag is covering your hand the whole time. After you pick it up you turn the bag inside out like this." I showed her by using the bag to pick up a little bundle of weeds. Then I emptied out the weeds and handed the bag to her. "Now try," I urged her. I really needed Lucy to get over this stumbling block today. If we wanted to launch Four Paws successfully, we couldn't have one of our dog walkers be unable to pick up dog poop.

"But what if there's a hole in the bag?" Lucy asked worriedly.

"There won't be a hole."

"Are you sure?"

"I'm positive," I lied. I mean, how could I know that? But it's just one of those things where you hope for the best.

Lucy put her hand inside the doggie bag. She closed her eyes and felt around in the grass, then gave up, opened her eyes, and scooped the poop.

"Great!" I said. "Now turn it inside out . . . good . . . tie the knot—you did it!"

Looking up at me with a smile, Lucy held the bag out like she wanted me to take it. "What do we do with it now?"

"*You* carry it. Until we find a trash can to toss it in."

Lucy held the bag away from her as we walked, but while she was so focused on staying far away from the poop bag, she let go of Meatball's leash, and he began trotting away from us.

"Oh no, Meatball!" I yelled, running up and bending over to catch his leash. "Whew." I stopped, gripping the end of his leash tightly and letting out a relieved breath.

"Oh, Kat—I'm sorry!" Lucy called. "I was just . . . I don't know what happened."

"Okay, amendment. Using the poop bag is now rule number two. Rule number one is absolutely this: Don't *ever* let go of the leash."

Lucy was staring at me with a strange expression on her face, and then she started laughing hysterically. Her face was even turning pink.

"Honestly, Luce, I don't think Meatball running away from us is funny . . ."

"It's . . . it's not that!" she gasped. "It's what . . . you said! Rule . . . number *two*! Get it?"

At the exact moment that I got it I started laughing, too. "Crap, I didn't mean that," I said, and then we both started laughing harder. We laughed all the way to the nearest garbage can, with a very confused Meatball looking up at me like, *What's with you?* I swear, he would look at me sometimes, and I just knew what my furry little friend wanted to say. I kept a tight hold on his leash the rest of the way home.

"How'd I do?" Lucy asked me when we reached the Burgundy.

"Pretty well!" I told her. "You might need a little more practice, but I think you're ready to become an official dog walker."

"I hope so," Lucy said, leaning down to scratch Meatball's ears while his tail wagged happily. "If only all dogs were as easy as Meatball. Thanks for being patient with me," she told him.

"It's true. Meatball is the best," I said with a sigh. I was a little sad to have to return him to Sarah and Dan, but soon enough, I knew, I'd be getting in more time with other dogs, even if they couldn't all be Meatball.

6
Not It

"Ta-da!" Taz announced on Monday morning, stopping at my locker after homeroom. She held in her hand the first Four Paws flyer. The logo on top was a number four with a drawing of a puppy paw behind it. The flyer read:

Introducing Four Paws Dog-Walking Agency!
For all your dog-walking needs, right here in the Burgundy!

Taz had drawn the flyer in shades of black and dark green,

which were the colors of the Burgundy's awning. It was really simple but eye-catching. It was so Taz to come up with just the right image on her first try.

"I love it!" I said.

"I'm glad," Taz said, admiring her handiwork. "It *is* really cool. We could even get T-shirts made with our logo. Or maybe hats. I look good in a hat."

"Of *course* you do," I said, and rolled my eyes as Taz laughed. "What's this bar code thing here?" I pointed to the bottom of the flyer.

"You scan it with your phone—I still need to add that direction on the flyer. It takes you to the app I set up. It's for scheduling," she explained. "Once a client joins, they can request a walk, a time, even a specific walker. They can also specify if it's a short walk or an exercise walk, and pay right there."

"Seriously? Taz, you're amazing!"

"I know. So where's Lucy? I wanted to show her the flyer, too."

"I haven't seen her yet," I said.

Meanwhile, I was looking all around for Declan, the new

boy I'd met on Friday. I hadn't seen him in the Burgundy all weekend, although I'd definitely been keeping my eyes peeled.

"Who are *you* looking for?" Taz asked. Trust Taz to not miss anything. My eyes swiveled back to her. Probably with a guilty expression in them. I hadn't actually found a chance to mention Declan to either of my best friends.

"There's a new boy in our grade," I said. "He lives in the Burgundy. I met him on Friday."

Taz perked up. "That's exciting. We haven't gotten a new kid in a while. How come you didn't tell us?"

"Well, I've been distracted launching our brand-new business."

"Hmm," Taz said, as though she didn't quite believe me. "He's in our grade, and lives in our building, and you didn't mention it?"

I decided to try to ignore her suspicion. "His name is Declan Ward," I said.

"Is he Irish? I think *Declan* is an Irish name."

"His dad is—accent and everything."

Taz's eyes widened. "You met his *dad*, too?"

"Just for a *minute*."

"Something's up with you, Cabot. You're not usually this cagey."

"Nothing is up!" I said, but my voice came out screechy.

Lucy appeared beside us. "What'd I miss?"

"Kat here met a boy on Friday and didn't tell either of us about it. Unless she told *you*."

Lucy glanced at me. "What? Nope—she didn't tell me *anything*. Kat, you mean you already met the new kid?"

"What new kid?" asked a lower voice from behind me. I jumped and let out a little shriek.

Taz and Lucy started laughing. I turned to see that, of course, Declan was standing behind me.

"We met in Drama Club this morning," Lucy said, looking smug. "Declan here just told me that he met *you* on Friday," she added.

Declan was in Drama Club? "I, um, I must have forgotten . . ." I began.

Declan put a hand in front of his heart and made a noise

like I'd shot an arrow into it. "Oof. I must have made a real big impression."

I was definitely blushing. "No, I mean—you did, I just . . ."

Declan's eyes were sparkling.

"Taz, this is Declan," Lucy was saying. "He's in our grade. And he lives in the Burgundy. But I guess Kat told you that. Just now," she added with a smirk.

Why oh why were my friends torturing me like this?

I felt my face turn even redder. "I'm sorry, Declan," I said. "It's just, right after I met you, I had the most amazing idea. It came from something that your dad said, actually. About your needing help walking Sparky."

"Is Sparky your dog?" Lucy asked.

Declan nodded. "A puppy, actually. I just got her. She's a pug."

"Kat's favorite," Taz threw in.

"What was your idea?" Declan asked me.

"I'm—we're—starting a dog-walking business! At the Burgundy." I showed Declan Taz's flyer.

Declan's eyes widened. "Whoa. That's a great idea. My dad

will be excited. When I go to my mom's I can't take Sparky since Mom's allergic."

"Oh, do you live with her half-time?" I asked.

Lucy gave me a look like maybe I was being too nosy asking that, but it was too late since I'd already asked. Also, I really wanted to know.

"No, just for one weekend a month. She lives in Philadelphia."

"Ah. Philly's cool," I added, not really sure what to say. Even though my parents were together, I knew how hard it was to be away from one parent a lot, because my dad traveled basically all the time.

"Not as cool as New York," Declan said, and I knew right then and there that in addition to being cute he was also 100 percent awesome.

The bell rang. Taz and Lucy had social studies together, and it turned out Declan and I were in the same English class. We walked there together.

"Come on," I told Declan. "I'll introduce you to Ms. Levine. She's really nice." I led Declan over to our teacher and said, "Ms. L, this is Declan—he's new."

Ms. Levine looked up from her computer. "Oh, hi! I got an email about a new student." She half stood out of her chair and shook Declan's hand. "Welcome. You can sit anywhere—there aren't any assigned seats. I'll see if I can find you a book for today's lesson, but until then, can you share with Kat?"

"Sure," Declan said.

"I usually sit over here," I told him, gesturing to the seat I'd already assigned myself by the wall.

"Thanks," Declan said. "I'm glad I met you on Friday. It's nice to have someone to show you around and stuff."

"Well, it seems like you would have met Lucy in drama this morning anyway," I said, unsure why that thought made me feel a little bit annoyed. "Are you really into that stuff?" I asked as we took our seats. "Acting?"

Declan frowned. "I don't know about *really* into. My mom's an actor, so I think it makes her happy that I'm at least trying it out."

"Oh, that's cool. I might want to go into business someday. Like my dad."

"I guess 'someday' is already here," Declan said with a smile. "I mean, since you're starting your own business."

"Yeah, I guess so," I said. The late bell rang and Ms. Levine started class.

I snuck a look over at Declan. He was just as cute under the fluorescent lights of the classroom as he had been in the lobby of the Burgundy on Friday.

It wasn't easy, but I dragged my attention back to Ms. Levine.

"In formal grammar," she was saying, "the word *it* is supposed to be used to refer to animals." But then she pointed to the picture of her dog, Oscar, behind her desk and said that she would *never* call him an *it*.

At that moment, even though the school year was very new, Ms. Levine quickly shot to the top of my favorite-teacher list.

After school, Lucy, Taz, and I gathered in my bedroom for the second official meeting of Four Paws Dog-Walking Agency. Mom had taken Micki to buy new shoes, so we had the apartment to ourselves. Taz had revised the flyer, made photocopies, *and* provided the snacks: a plate of her mom's delicious samosas.

"These are amazing," I said, taking a big bite of the hot, flaky treat. Lucy nodded in agreement, her mouth full.

"You know it," Taz said, polishing off her own samosa. "So what's next?"

"I was thinking we could hang up the flyers in the laundry room on each floor," I said, wiping my hands with a napkin.

"Good idea," Lucy said. "Should we start on the top floor and work our way down?"

"I already put one in the laundry room on my floor," said Taz, who lived on the tenth floor.

"Okay," I said. "Let's start on nine, then."

We were waiting for the elevator (and it was taking forever as usual) when Taz said, "I wonder which floor Declan's on."

"He's on four," Lucy said before I could answer. "He told me in Drama Club."

The elevator finally arrived and we stepped inside.

"What's wrong?" Lucy asked me.

"What, why?"

"You're frowning."

"Oh. I was just thinking about how much homework I have to do later," I lied.

I couldn't tell my best friend that I was feeling jealous for no

57

reason about Declan. It wasn't like I could have hoped to be the only one who knew him. He lived in our building, and he went to our school.

And of *course* he hit it off with Lucy. She was beautiful and nice and funny. I couldn't hold it against him for having good taste.

We got off on the ninth floor and walked into the laundry room. Like all the laundry rooms, this one had a big corkboard hanging on the wall, so it was easy to figure out where to put the flyer. I scanned the rest of the board. There were ads for babysitters, tutors, housekeepers, and giveaways of furniture. But no other ads for dog walkers. I let out a sigh of relief. My dad always said that a big part of business was finding the right untapped market.

I used one of the pushpins on the board to tack up a flyer. It looked great up there—attention-grabbing and fun.

"Do you think we'll get bombarded with a lot of clients right away?" I asked my friends hopefully.

"I don't know," Lucy said. "I figured we'd probably start with just one or two dogs."

"Yeah, we have to keep our expectations realistic," Taz said, and I nodded, feeling worried. What if *nobody* contacted us? I tried to push the thought away.

To save time, the three of us decided to split up the rest of the floors and meet back at my apartment when we were done. Lucy would do floors six, seven, and eight, Taz would do floors two and one, and I quickly volunteered to do floors three, four, and five, since five was my floor, after all. And okay, maybe I secretly really wanted the fourth floor.

Still, I told myself as I walked down the stairs, what were the chances that I'd even see Declan?

I started on the third floor, posted the flyer on the corkboard there, and then went up the stairs to four. I walked into the laundry room and almost ran right into Declan. Which prompted me to drop the flyers I was carrying.

"Hi!" I said, starting to bend down to pick up the scattered flyers. Declan bent down, too, and we cracked our heads together with a loud thwack.

We both reeled back, exclaiming, "Ow!"

"I'm so sorry!" I said.

"Don't apologize—we ran into each other," Declan said,

rubbing his head. "I'm going to kneel down now. You"—he put up a palm—"you stay there. Okay?"

"Okay. Thank you," I said, feeling awkward as he picked up the scattered flyers, then stood up to hand them to me. "Thanks again," I said. "And I'm sorry about your brain."

"It's not my best feature," he joked. But since I still felt embarrassed, I forgot to laugh. "I was *going* to say that my best feature was my sense of humor, but . . . maybe not."

This time I laughed, rubbing my own head. "I'm sure it is when your audience doesn't have a super-recent brain injury."

Declan let out a laugh. "See, now, *that's* funny!"

I smiled. Making him laugh made me feel much cooler all of a sudden.

"So, have you found any customers yet?" Declan asked, nodding at the flyers.

"Well, Sparky, hopefully," I said.

I guess she heard her name, because a tiny white pug head pushed up out of the big basket of laundry at Declan's feet. She gave a short, friendly-sounding bark as though she were saying hi to me. "Oh my goodness!" I exclaimed, dropping down to my knees to pet her silky head and ears. "Declan, she's just too cute for words."

"I know," Declan said. "I wasn't going to bring her to the laundry room with me, but she makes this sad face whenever I start to leave her."

"Awww," I said, giving her a kiss on the top of her head. "Of course she does."

"I'll definitely mention Four Paws to my dad," Declan said. "I'm going to visit my mom in a few weeks, so I'm sure he'll need the extra help."

"Great! And if you don't mind, maybe you could spread the word on your floor?" I was still scratching Sparky's ears. She had her eyes closed in puppy bliss.

"I don't know anybody yet, but I'll look out for opportunities," Declan said. "Hey, Kat, can I ask you something?" he added, suddenly sounding nervous.

My cheeks for sure turned not just pink but probably red, and my heartbeat sped up. What did he want to ask?

"Um, sure," I said, giving Sparky one last pat and standing up to face Declan.

"I was wondering if you'd mind if I walked to school with you and your friends sometime?"

Oh! That made sense. What had I been thinking he would ask, anyway? That he would ask me out, like, on a date? I almost laughed at myself.

"Of course!" I said. "But I have to warn you, my little sister, Micki, comes as part of the package."

"I'm happy to meet more people. Even little sisters," he said with a smile. Then he glanced down at the laundry basket. "I guess I should get back to the laundry here. Don't want my dad to say I've made a hames of it."

"You don't want him to say you made ham?" I asked, frowning.

"Sorry, it's just a bit of Irish slang. You'll get used to it, lass," he added in his dad's accent.

I laughed. "Got it." I tacked the flyer up on the corkboard, and Declan waved as he carried the basket over to the nearest washing machine. Sparky gave a little good-bye bark.

I left the laundry room and it took me a full ten seconds to remember where I was going next.

After I hung up the flyer in my laundry room, I decided to make a special visit to the Thompsons and give them their flyer in person. I rang their doorbell, and when Dan opened the door, Meatball heard my voice and came barreling toward me on his adorable short legs.

"Meatball!" I knelt down right away to give him some petting. He rolled right over onto his back so I would rub his belly.

"I swear that dog likes you better than it likes me," Dan said.

He, I corrected in my head. *Not* it.

"I doubt that," I said, even though I secretly hoped it was true. I stood up and handed Dan a flyer. "This is a new dog-walking business my friends and I are starting," I explained. "You can use the app to book appointments for me—um, for any of us—to walk Meatball."

"Sure," Dan said, studying the flyer. "I think Sarah mentioned to me that you'd be doing this. Sounds great. We need all the help we can get." Behind Dan, I heard a crash, and one of the twins started crying. Dan sighed.

"Are you looking forward to our walks, boy?" I asked Meatball.

He looked up at me, his butt wiggling happily, and I swear he smiled.

7
Ding!

Ding.

I looked up from my homework. Another notification from the Four Paws schedule app had just come through on my phone.

After a slow start the first week, suddenly Four Paws was being bombarded with requests. It was very exciting. Taz, Lucy, and I were taking several dogs on walks nearly every afternoon. We had all kinds of dogs: Mary-Kate and Ashley, the Yorkie sisters from the second floor; Kekáki, a round little dachshund from the tenth floor; Rufus the labradoodle, also from the tenth floor; Biscuit, who was part mastiff but I wasn't sure what else, from the seventh floor; Batman and Robin, the border collies, from the third floor; and Wendy the Westie from the first floor.

We'd even had requests for early morning walks, but so far I was the only one who'd been willing to get up forty-five minutes early to walk someone else's dog before school.

I checked the latest request—it was from Kekáki's owner, asking if one of us could do a walk tomorrow afternoon. Taz had set up the app so that any one of us could claim a request. I quickly accepted this one for myself. I put my phone down and turned back to my homework, but then my phone buzzed with a text from Lucy.

Kat I have to turn off the 🔔 from the app=driving me crazy! Can you just text me if you need me to do a walk??

I frowned. I kind of got it—the notifications were a lot. But it wasn't my job to claim walks for Lucy. What if I said yes to one when she ended up having Drama Club, or something with her mom?

Luce you have to claim the walks yourself. Mute it and check every couple hours if you want. K?

A few minutes later I got back a sad face emoji followed by a thumbs-up.

"Kat! Dinner!" Mom called.

"Coming!" I yelled back. I put my phone in my pocket and ran to the kitchen. "Do you need me to do anything?" I asked Mom.

"Nope, have a seat. We're just having a casserole."

"Not that tuna one?" I asked.

"You got lucky. It's chicken. Now, sit."

I slid into my usual chair and took the plate Mom handed to me. I tried to pass it to Micki, but she had her tablet out and was watching some video with the volume off.

"Mick, you know the rules—devices away at the table," Mom said.

Micki let out a grumbly sigh and put her tablet aside. She accepted the plate I gave her, then leaned over to me. "I came this close to a yes to eating in the living room," she whispered loudly.

"I went to the trouble of cooking, so we're eating at the table. Like civilized people." Mom handed me my plate and then went back to scoop up some casserole for herself. I looked down dubiously at my plate. Mom's cooking was kind of a hit-or-miss thing. At first glance this looked like a miss.

Mom sat down with her plate, lifted a forkful to her mouth, and then jumped a little when my phone dinged again. "Micki, what did I . . ."

I put a hand up. "No—it's me. Sorry. It's another notification for Four Paws. We're having trouble keeping up with demand. Who knew there were so many people who didn't want to walk their own dogs?"

"Kat, it's not about wanting," Mom chided me. "Your dog walking is taking off because people don't always have time to spend with the people—or pets—that they love."

Hmm. Why had Mom put it that way? Was she feeling guilty? Or was she thinking about Dad, who was still away?

"I know," I told Mom. "I was joking." I took a cautious bite of the chicken casserole. Mmm. It was much better than expected. "We're just so busy," I added. "I even have to take Batman and Robin out tonight after dinner!"

"And after homework, yes?" Mom reminded me, and I

nodded. That was the rule. "Maybe you need to recruit another walker," Mom added, taking a sip of water. "If it's too much for the three of you to manage."

"I could do it!" Micki said.

"No!" both Mom and I said at the same time. But it was to me that Micki turned her sad eyes and hurt expression.

"I'd do a good job," she protested.

"I know you would," I said. "You're just too young for people to hire you to look after their pets. I mean, it's a lot like babysitting. People's dogs are like their babies."

Micki turned to Mom next. "What she said," Mom said around a mouthful of chicken.

Micki let out a frustrated sigh and threw her fork down on her plate. "Can I be excused?"

"After that thimbleful of dinner you just ate? No, try again. Tell me about your day."

"What's a thimble?" Micki asked.

Mom sighed. "You use it in sewing. In other news, I am one hundred years old."

I let out a laugh, but Micki still looked confused.

"I only know what thimbles are from Nana," I explained. "She gave me this little sewing kit when I was your age, and she told me how to use everything in it."

"I've never seen you sew, Kat," Mom said.

I shook my head. "I never did. But I guess I could. I mean, if I could remember where I put that kit."

Now Mom let out a chuckle.

Micki had eaten some more casserole. "*Now* can I be excused?"

"Sure," Mom said. She peered at my empty plate. "*You* must have been hungry?"

"It was good," I told her. "Really good."

Mom smiled. "Thanks."

After I'd helped Mom clear the table and finished my homework, I took the stairs down to the third floor and knocked on the Crowleys' door.

"Hi, Kat," said Mrs. Crowley as Batman and Robin raced over, leaping and barking. I usually liked smaller dogs best, but these two border collies had the sweetest faces. "Here are their leashes. Robin's a little feisty. Are you sure you can handle both of them at one time?" I knew Taz had walked Batman and Robin last week, but I didn't know if she'd taken the siblings out separately.

I considered. "Well, why don't I try it, at least to go across the street, and if I have a problem, I can come back up and we'll do one at a time?"

"Sounds good," Mrs. Crowley said.

"Hi, guys," I said, petting Robin on the head. She had a pink collar, while Batman's was blue.

I could see why Mrs. Crowley had warned me—Robin tried to go after everything we passed by, from fire hydrants to other dogs. But Batman seemed to actually calm her down, and she would fall into step with her brother whenever we stopped and I said her name. I decided to make a note for the other Paws: Walk the superhero and the sidekick *together*.

"Come *on*, Kekáki!"

The next afternoon, I was tugging lightly on the leash of my latest client, but he just didn't want to budge. *Kekáki* means "cupcake" in Greek, according to his owner, Mrs. Galanis. I guess naming him after a dessert destined him to be a very round little dachshund. His long belly almost touched the sidewalk when we walked. But at the moment, we weren't walking. Kekáki had just flopped down on the sidewalk and looked up at me with his tongue hanging out.

I knew from walking Kekáki earlier in the week that the little dachshund was very lazy. I wasn't even taking him all the way to the dog park, like we did for most of our clients. The park was too far for this little cupcake to walk. But today he was being even lazier than usual, refusing to even make a move toward the nearest patch of grass. I gazed down at him, and he gave me a please-pet-my-belly? look. I sighed and knelt down to give him a few pats. His tail wagged happily.

I looked across the street and saw Marcel open the door for someone at the Burgundy. A few seconds later, I saw Lucy step outside, walking—wait, why was Lucy walking *Meatball*?

"Hey! Good timing. We can walk together!" Lucy called when she saw me with Kekáki. She crossed the street and joined us.

"I didn't know Meatball was signed up for a walk today?" I tried to keep my voice casual, but I couldn't help feeling upset. I knew Four Paws was a business, and you're supposed to be objective when it comes to business. But I *always* walked Meatball.

"Oh, Sarah caught me in the elevator a few minutes ago and asked me."

I nodded. "That makes sense. I didn't think I saw him on the schedule."

"Of course not. Otherwise you would have signed yourself up to walk him," Lucy said, but then she laughed.

I smiled sheepishly. Lucy was right; I did always rush to claim Meatball for walks. I gave Meatball a kiss on the top of his head before standing up. "I'm sorry. I can't help playing favorites when it comes to this little guy."

"I know," Lucy said. Meatball strained forward on his leash, clearly eager to get to the dog park. "Should we get going?" Lucy asked. "Sarah said Dan Jr. has an appointment so I can't be long with Meatball."

I gestured down to Kekáki, who had rolled back over onto

his stomach and closed his eyes, looking for all the world like he was about to take a nap right there on the sidewalk. "You go ahead," I told Lucy. "I don't think any forward motion will be happening with this one anytime soon."

"Okay," Lucy said. "But if you want to switch . . ."

"No, don't be silly. Sarah knows you took Meatball out. We have to be professional. But still, thanks for asking." I smiled.

"Sure thing, bestie. Hey, I'll text you tonight, 'kay?" she said. "Mom's taking me to a thrift store to find the perfect outfit. Auditions start next week!"

"Oh, that's right," I said. I'd forgotten the fall play was coming up soon.

I waved to Meatball and Lucy as they trotted off, then returned my focus to my client. The lazy cupcake was almost fast asleep at my feet.

"Time for desperate measures," I announced, reaching into my pocket and pulling out the small plastic bag of treats I'd started carrying on my dog walks. "Now, Kekáki," I said, leaning down, "if you make your business, you can have this entire meaty cookie. Okay?"

I swear he understood. Dachshunds are very food motivated—and very smart. He lumbered to his feet, ambled over to the grass, and got down to business.

"Hooray!" I said, giving him his reward. We waited for a few cars to pass, then crossed the street back to our building.

"Hard at work, Kat?" Marcel asked me.

"I sure am," I told him. "I wish the weather would finally get a little cooler."

Marcel pretended to mop his brow. "You and me both!" he said, and I laughed. "Why aren't you walking Meatball? He's your favorite, isn't he?"

I explained how I'd claimed Kekáki for a walk first, then smiled to myself. I guessed everyone knew Meatball was my favorite. There was no point in hiding it, really. If I could have any dog of my very own, I'd pick one exactly like him.

Once I returned Kekáki, I went back to my apartment. Mom had taken Micki to a pool party; one of the girls in Micki's grade had a pool in her building's gym, and it was Micki's favorite thing in the world. She'd been asking our parents if we could get a pool for the past year, which made me giggle since we lived in a pretty small apartment. The bathtub was definitely as close as Mick was ever going to get.

I walked around the empty apartment, feeling lonely all of a sudden. Lucy would soon be off shopping for an audition costume, and Taz was with one of her sisters doing some kind of paint night. And I knew Declan and his dad were having dinner with some friends of Mr. Ward's from work; Declan had mentioned it on our walk to school that morning. He'd been walking with me, Lucy, Taz, and Micki almost every morning, and he'd fit in really easily.

I flopped into my favorite chair in the silent living room. Even though I missed my friends, I realized there was someone in particular I wanted to talk to. I opened up my phone and started writing a text to my dad. I had so much I wanted to ask him about my new business. Before long, my questions filled almost the entire screen. Then I paused. I knew how busy Dad was on this business trip. And I also knew he'd probably take a long time to write me back, and that when he did he'd just say something short like, *Talk when I get home.*

That thought was just too depressing to even consider, so I highlighted the whole text and deleted it.

Just then our Four Paws app dinged again, for a last-minute walk, and this time I was happy for the distraction. I put my shoes back on and went to get Mary-Kate and Ashley.

8

Rocket Girl

I woke up at 6:15 A.M. the next day to walk Mary-Kate and Ashley *again*. Their mom, Charlotte, was quickly becoming one of our biggest clients. Today she was leaving on an early flight, and her dog sitter wasn't going to be able to come until later in the day.

The walk was quick and easy—Mary-Kate and Ashley were older, so they were mellow and obedient. When I got back home, I picked up my phone, went into our app, and marked the walk completed. I saw that Charlotte had already sent us the payment.

At this rate, Taz would have her tablet and Lucy would have her acting class in no time.

I only hoped that both my friends would still want to be part of the business once they'd reached their goals. There was no way I could keep up with all the demand myself at this point.

I poured myself a bowl of cereal, ate it, and went to wake up Micki for school. When the two of us got down into the lobby, Lucy, Taz, and Declan were waiting. They were talking excitedly about the school's fall play.

"Basically, I *have* to get Emily," Lucy was saying. "I mean, a lot of plays have more than one great female character. But not really this one. My other options here are the two moms. No thank you."

Declan laughed. "You're right. I hadn't even thought of it that way. But hey, is there any reason the Stage Manager character *has* to be a guy?"

Lucy's eyes lit up. "You're right . . . I mean—hey, Kat. Hey, Micki—I don't know if being the narrator is really my style, but it is a *huge* part . . ."

"What play are they doing this year?" I asked as we all waved to Marcel and walked outside.

"Didn't you hear?" Lucy said. "We're doing *Our Town*. It was posted outside Mr. Cornell's office yesterday."

Since I didn't take drama and had never even stepped inside Mr. Cornell's classroom, I definitely hadn't paid any attention to what he'd posted outside his room.

"That's cool," I said. "We're reading that in English this year."

Micki fell into step beside me and tapped me on the arm. "Kat, I forgot my lunch," she said.

"I set it out for you," I told her, trying not to roll my eyes. We didn't have time to go back to the apartment, and Micki was a pretty picky eater. I knew the odds that she'd eat whatever they had in the cafeteria today were pretty small.

"I know but I forgot to grab it."

I frowned. I didn't exactly love the cafeteria food, either. "I brought the same thing for myself," I told her. "You can have my lunch." I unzipped my backpack, pulled out my lunch bag, and handed it to her.

"Thanks, Kat!" Micki said as she took it from me and skipped ahead happily.

Declan was sort of staring at me. I almost felt like I was about to blush again when Lucy said, "Micki's lucky she has a big sister to bail her out all the time. Sometimes it's hard being an only."

I felt like saying that sometimes it's kind of rough being the oldest, too—like right now. But I didn't. "Do you have money for lunch?" Declan asked me.

"We can get it on credit at school. But thank you," I added, smiling at him. He smiled back.

When we got to school, we all headed for our separate home-rooms. Once homeroom started, Mrs. Jackson read out a list of announcements in her usual loud, monotone voice. "Auditions will be held for the fall play beginning on Tuesday. Sign-up sheets are outside Mr. Cornell's classroom. Today's lunch menu is meat loaf, cauliflower puree, and kale salad."

I tried not to groan aloud at that. School meat loaf *and* cauliflower puree? Micki really had picked a terrific day to forget her lunch. I thought longingly of the nice, plain turkey sandwich I'd packed. Mom often said I wasn't a very adventurous eater. I could live with that.

When I got to English class I looked around for Declan, but the bell was about to ring and he wasn't there. What if he'd switched classes? I frowned and picked at a nick at the edge of my grammar book's spine.

But then, just as the bell was ringing, he slid into the seat beside me, out of breath.

"What happened?" I asked him.

"Just got a little turned around," he told me.

That seemed weird, since Declan had mentioned the other day, on the walk to school, that he had a really good sense of direction. But I let it go. Ms. Levine had put up a slideshow about *Our Town* and wanted us to take notes. It sounded like a pretty interesting story. I wondered if Lucy would get the lead like she hoped, or maybe play that narrator part she and Declan had been talking about this morning.

Lunch period finally came, and I walked up to the line to sign in for a lunch on credit. But Declan came up to me and handed me a small white paper bag.

"What's this?" I asked, looking down at it in confusion.

"Come on, let's grab a table and you can find out."

"But I . . ." I gestured to the lunch line.

"Come on," Declan said with a mischievous smile. "Trust me." I noticed he was holding an identical white paper bag of his own. Mysterious.

I followed him to our usual table, where Taz was already sitting with her lunch.

Declan and I both sat down. I opened the bag Declan had handed to me, unwrapped the foil packet inside, and saw: a turkey sandwich!

I looked up at Declan. "How did you know? And how did you do this?"

Declan grinned. "My dad had to come in and drop off a school medical form for me, so I texted him to ask if he could pick up some food, too. And after homeroom, I ran down to your sister's classroom and asked what you had packed, so I could text my dad to bring the same. And it sounded good, so I asked for one for myself, too."

"That's so nice of you!" I said, feeling my face break into a giant grin. My day had just gone from disappointing to pretty awesome. It wasn't just about having a good lunch. I also felt happy that Declan had done something so sweet. For me.

Taz was giving me a look, but I tried to ignore it.

Lucy sat down with her lunch tray. She'd skipped the meat loaf but gotten the cauliflower and salad. I wondered if she was going vegetarian again, or if I should offer her half of my turkey sandwich.

"Are you okay eating that?" I asked her.

"What? Oh, I'm not really hungry—Mom made me a breakfast burrito this morning. But, guys, listen. I heard that the only eighth grader signed up to audition for George right now is *Mitchell Brown*. I mean, I know I'm not a lock for Emily. Both Shelby Firestone and Misty Carmichael are definitely auditioning for Emily, too. But if I do get it . . ." Lucy turned to Declan and grabbed on to his sleeve. "Declan, you *have* to audition to be George."

"I was actually thinking of trying out, but I'd like to play the Stage Manager."

Lucy frowned. "I thought you said a girl should play that."

"Well, I was just saying that the part *could* be played by a girl," Declan said. "But it's the part I'd like the best, I think. I read most of the play last night."

Wow, I thought. We hadn't even gotten our copies for class yet.

"Please, please, *please*, Declan—you have to do it. In the play Emily gets *married* to George. I *cannot* marry Mitchell Brown, even just onstage. It's just, no."

The thought of Lucy and Declan getting married—even just onstage—made me kind of upset for some reason.

"I guess I could try out for George, too," Declan said, and Lucy squealed in delight.

I looked down at my turkey sandwich, and suddenly I wasn't all that hungry anymore.

After school, I waited for Taz and Lucy in my room to begin our Four Paws meeting.

Lucy showed up first. Instead of taking her usual spot on the beanbag chair near my closet door, she flopped onto my bed. "I am in for a long night memorizing lines," she announced. "Auditions are on Tuesday. I've *got* to get the part of Emily."

"You'll get it. You got one of the lead roles last year," I reminded her. "Besides, you're the best actress at our school."

Lucy rolled over to face me. "You have to say that because you're my best friend."

"I mean, yeah, but that doesn't mean it's not true. Ask Taz, then. You know she'll give you the truth."

"Whether you want it or not," Lucy agreed with a smile. Taz was known for her radical honesty. Just then the doorbell rang, and I jumped up to answer the door. But Micki was already letting Taz into the apartment.

"Does everyone else have a ridiculous amount of homework tonight for some reason?" Taz asked, slumping into a chair in the living room.

"We're having the meeting in my room," I reminded her.

Taz groaned. "But this chair is so comfy," she protested.

I pulled her up by her arm. "Come *on*. Go grab whatever you want to drink out of the fridge. I've got the snacks all ready."

"Ooh, what snacks?" Micki asked.

"The same thing I already gave you for your snack," I told

my sister. "Cookies. You can't have double snack—you'll never eat your dinner."

"Fine by me. So when can I join Four Paws?"

"When you're older," I told her as Taz went into the kitchen and grabbed some juice. "Besides, what happened to you always wanting to have cats? You always used to say you wanted to have five cats when you got older. Exactly five. No dogs."

Micki's face scrunched up as she considered. "I think that might be too many. And I think now I want a puppy, too."

"Glad you're finally seeing sense and becoming a dog person," I said.

"So can I join Four Paws, then?" my little sister prompted.

"God, Mick, I said no. Now stop hounding me!" I said in a frustrated voice.

Micki's face fell, and she turned and walked back to her room without saying anything.

"Kind of harsh," truth-telling Taz said from the kitchen. But I didn't need anybody else to tell me I'd just made my little sister feel bad. "Do you want to go talk to her?" Taz asked, coming over to me.

I shook my head. "She's sulking now. It wouldn't do any good. I'll just have to find a way to make it up to her. Besides, we should get through the meeting."

Lucy was reading her printout of the *Our Town* script when Taz and I walked into the bedroom. She looked super stressed. Suddenly I felt guilty for insisting we have a meeting today. I knew Taz was stressed about her homework, too.

"Hey, guys," I announced, and my friends looked at me. "Unless there's anything pressing you want to talk about, we can postpone this meeting until next week."

I held my breath in case Taz or maybe even Lucy hassled me for calling the meeting and then canceling it. But both were nodding, and Lucy was standing up and putting her script back into her bag. "That'd be great, Kat," Lucy said. "Oh, I did want to tell you—if I get the part, I won't be able to go on nearly as many dog walks."

"And I'm going to offer to do the costumes for the play," Taz said, sounding guilty.

"Okay," I said, trying not to panic.

"We'll work it out," Taz said.

"Sure," I told them. "Hey, grab some snacks if you want."

Taz and Lucy took some of the cookies I'd put out and headed toward my bedroom door.

"Later, Kat!" they both called.

I walked out into the quiet apartment after my friends had gone. I stood outside my sister's door. Sulking or no, I knew I had to try to make things better.

I knocked but she didn't answer, so I opened her door. "Hey, Micki," I called, but she was wearing her big headphones and looking down at her tablet. I walked over and waved my hand in front of the screen and she jumped.

"You scared me!"

"Sorry."

"Aren't you busy having your big meeting?"

"We're finished. Besides, I wanted to come check on you. And to say I'm sorry I snapped at you."

"Okay. Thanks." Micki started to put her headphones back on.

"Hey, wait! I was also coming to see if you wanted to have a sister day on Saturday."

Micki narrowed her eyes a bit. "What do you mean, a 'sister day'?"

"I mean, like a day to spend together, just the two of us. We can do whatever you want, even."

Micki's eyes went wide. "Really? Like, anything?"

I started to feel a little scared. "I mean, within reason. I can't afford *Harry Potter and the Cursed Child* tickets." Micki and I both adored all things Harry Potter but hadn't been able to see the Broadway play yet. "And nothing we're not allowed to do," I added, "like go all the way to New Jersey by ourselves."

"I wasn't thinking of either of those things. I want to go to a museum."

This was news to me. Micki had never shown any interest in art up until now.

"Great! Which one?"

"It's called the Intrepid."

"Isn't that the big boat down on Pier 86?" I asked, confused. Micki wasn't into boats, either, as far as I knew.

"Yeah, but there's a whole museum there—it's got sea, air, *and* space. It's the space part I want to see. They have the *Enterprise*."

"Like in the movies?"

"No, silly. It's named after *Star Trek*, but it was the first proto-type space shuttle. I really want to see it. We learned all about the space program in science."

I looked at my sister and for the first time noticed that she was wearing earrings shaped like moons and stars, and that the T-shirt she'd been wearing the most lately, and was wearing now, had a *Star Trek* logo on it. "When did you get so into space stuff?"

Micki raised her eyebrows at me and frowned. "Um, *last* year. After having Mr. Sarles for science. He turned his class-room into a planetarium—it was so cool!"

I felt so clueless for not realizing that my little sister had been sort of obsessed with space for almost a year. "The Intrepid sounds great," I said. "I mean, I need to check with Mom. But in the meantime, why don't you go online and see if we need special tickets for the exhibit?"

Without warning, Micki lurched up off her bed and wrapped her arms around me. "Thanks, Kat," she said before letting go. Then she picked up her tablet and pulled up the Intrepid web-site, her eyes shining.

As I left Micki's room, Mom was opening up the front door. I went to tell her about my idea for a sister day. She looked at me with something like surprise on her face. It made me feel equal parts good and guilty—good for making Micki so happy, but guilty that Mom would be so surprised by the fact that I was doing it in the first place.

On Saturday morning, Mom, Micki, and I headed to the subway together. The plan was: Mom would ride the train to Midtown with us, but then Micki and I would walk over to the museum, just the two of us. When we were ready to leave the museum, I'd text Mom, and she'd meet us back at the subway station to go home.

"I think it's so nice you two are having a sister day," Mom said as we rode the train, her eyes going a little misty. "I always wished I had a sister, you know."

Micki gave me a smile and a gentle eye roll. We both knew all about Mom wishing for a sister. She got along well with her brother, Jason, our uncle. But she was always jealous that Dad had two sisters.

Finally we reached our stop. We said goodbye to Mom and headed off the train and out of the station. It was a long walk to the Intrepid, but Micki and I chatted the whole time. And when we got there, Micki was so excited while we waited in line that she was kind of dancing around. I wished for a moment that I felt that excited about something. I guessed that business was my *thing*, but it didn't exactly make me dance around. I did feel that excited to see Meatball, but I never danced—in fact I always tried to act calm and responsible.

Micki oohed and aahed all over the space shuttle prototype, and then I used some of the money Mom had given me to buy her a T-shirt that said ROCKET GIRL.

As we were walking back to the subway to meet Mom, Micki leaned her head on my shoulder and said, "Love you, sis."

At that moment, I felt like I was a hundred feet tall.

9

Sharing Sparky

"I still need colored pencils. *And* a blue and a red notebook," Micki announced at breakfast the next morning. Micki had been reminding Mom that she needed extra school supplies for the past two weeks.

Mom gave me a pleading look. "Do you have any dog walking today, Kat?" she asked.

I knew what Mom was getting at, and she was in luck. The Four Paws app had been relatively quiet, and I didn't have to do any walks until tomorrow.

"I'm free," I said, and I glanced over at Micki. It seemed our Sister Saturday was turning into a whole Sister Weekend.

I walked with Micki to a store in the neighborhood that sold stationery and school supplies. Micki was pushing the small cart, and as she rounded the corner into the notebook aisle she almost collided with another cart. The occupant of that cart's kiddie basket gave a short, high-pitched bark. I gasped. It was Sparky the pug puppy, wearing a tiny black T-shirt and looking up at me with her huge black eyes.

"Sparky!" I exclaimed, rushing forward to pet her.

"Nice to see *you* again, too, Kat," Declan said dryly. My eyes flew up to meet his, and I felt my cheeks go red.

"I'm sorry! Hi, Declan!"

"Getting some stuff for school?" he asked.

I nodded. "You, too?"

"Yep. I keep having to borrow people's pens so I figured I'd just get a bunch."

"Can I pet her?" Micki asked, pointing to Sparky.

"Sure. She's very friendly."

Hesitantly, Micki scratched Sparky's tiny ears. Sparky

wriggled around happily. It did seem that Micki was warming up to dogs.

"Good job finding the best place to buy stuff for school," I told Declan. "Mr. and Mrs. Levinson always give us extra stickers and they have a great selection of notebooks."

"Kat gets very nerdy about school supplies." Micki rolled her eyes at me as she petted Sparky.

"I just like to be organized," I defended myself.

"Nothing wrong with that," Declan said. "So do you two have any other places in the neighborhood to recommend?"

"So many," I said. "There's the Museum of Natural History and Central Park and Riverside Park. Oh, and Zabar's has the best bagels."

"The best place in the entire neighborhood is Amorino—it's a gelato place!" Micki exclaimed, looking up from Sparky.

"I love gelato," Declan said. "Where is it?"

"We can take you now!" Micki said, and I worked hard to not blush since she'd basically just invited both of us to go out for ice cream with Declan.

But Declan just smiled and said, "Sounds good to me."

"Can I go back and look at the markers one more time?" Micki asked me, and I nodded.

"Your sister seems to love dogs, too," Declan said.

"Yeah. I didn't know quite how much until she met Sparky, though," I said with a laugh.

Declan patted Sparky's head. "It's hard to resist Sparky. I can't believe my dad found her at a shelter."

"Really? I would have expected a purebred dog like her to come from a breeder."

"Och, noo—Sean Ward would ne'er do somethin' as socially irresponsible as that, lass," Declan said in another perfect imitation of his dad's accent. I laughed again. "I meant to ask," Declan added, "how come your parents don't let you and Micki have pets of your own?"

I frowned. "My dad's gone a lot for his job, and my mom works full-time and is really busy, too."

"That's a bummer, I'm sorry. But you can share Sparky, since we're neighbors."

"That would be amazing!" I told him. "I mean, you should be

careful offering to share one of the cutest puppies ever, though. What if I just went ahead and dog-napped her?"

"I'd never let Sparky get dog-napped," he said in a mock-fierce tone. "But what do you mean, 'one of the cutest'? Are you implying that Sparky is not the single cutest puppy you've ever seen?"

"Puppy? Yes. But don't forget about Meatball."

"Oh, right, how could I forget your favorite?"

"I think Sparky and Meatball should definitely meet up sometime," I said. "They are sure to love each other."

Declan grinned. "I'm sure Sparky could use another friend. Poor girl's just stuck with only me most of the time." Declan scratched his puppy's ears, and I sighed a little, thinking, *I wouldn't mind being stuck with you.*

I felt my cheeks turn pink again. I'd never been like this with any boy. I snuck another look at Declan. I knew I needed to be careful with my heart around a boy as cute as he was.

"What's the matter?" Declan asked.

"Nothing," I lied. "I was just thinking how cute Sparky and

Meatball will be together. Maybe I could get Meatball a shirt to match Sparky's. What's the logo on it?"

"Oh, my dad designed it. It's her name spelled out in runes. Dad's an artist, and folk symbols from ancient Ireland are kind of his thing."

"Never mind trying to match, then," I said with a laugh.

Micki came back then, holding a giant pack of markers. "Can I get this one?"

I took it from her hand and looked at the price tag. "Not unless you want to see Mom's head explode."

"Okay, how about this one?" Micki pulled a much smaller pack from behind her back. "It's only ten dollars."

"Smart kid," Declan said, giving Micki a wink, and she giggled.

"I guess so. Mick, we should pay if you still want to stop for gelato," I told her.

"Of course I do, jeez," Micki said, shaking her head and starting to push our little cart up to the front of the store.

"Unless you weren't done shopping?" I looked down at Declan's cart.

"I just need some mechanical pencils and I'm done," he said.

"I know right where those are," I said, motioning for him to follow. He picked a pack of six and then pushed his cart to the front, with me walking alongside. I stepped up to pay for Micki's and my supplies. The Levinsons' daughter was ringing us up, and I was afraid we wouldn't get any stickers, but I saw her smile at Micki and put a few sheets in the bag.

After Declan paid for his supplies, he insisted on carrying our bags along with his. Declan let Micki carry Sparky in her tiny dog-carrying bag after she promised to be careful. I kept worrying she would bump into somebody on the crowded sidewalk, since she kept putting her face down into the bag to talk to Sparky.

"One of the next generation of dog walkers for your business, right there," Declan said.

"Yeah, she keeps trying to join," I said.

"Don't look so horrified. She's doing a good job with Sparky."

"I guess so," I said doubtfully. I turned to look at him as we walked. "It's really nice of you to let Micki carry her, Declan. And to say we can share your puppy. Seeing you and Sparky really reminds me how much I want one of my own."

"Maybe you should ask your parents again. The holidays will be coming up before long."

"Yeah, maybe," I said, thinking that I'd need to wait until the next time Dad was home. I knew if I asked Mom she'd just say, *Wait until your father gets home.* It was her default setting on anything remotely major.

Amorino was less crowded than usual, so we got our gelato fast, and then of course we had to eat it fast, too, because it was still pretty hot outside.

All too soon we were back inside the Burgundy's lobby, and Declan was trading our shopping bags for Sparky's carrier. We rode the elevator up together, and he got off on the fourth floor and waved goodbye.

"I like him. He should be your boyfriend," Micki said after the doors closed.

"I know." The words slipped out before I had a chance to stop myself.

Micki turned to me, her mouth forming a surprised O. "You *like* like him!"

"It's more complicated than that, Mick," I told her, blushing furiously. "And you can't say anything to anybody—especially Declan himself, got it? He's . . . well, you can see how ridiculously cute he is. Odds are he wouldn't go for someone like me. So you have to *promise*." I tried to ignore the feeling of panic in my stomach as I imagined Declan finding out.

Micki frowned. "I don't see why he wouldn't like you." But then the elevator doors opened, and Micki spotted a man with a suitcase standing outside our door.

"Dad!" she yelled, and hurtled herself out of the elevator and into his arms.

10
Trying

"Hi, Dad," I said. After Micki finally let go of him, he pulled me forward and enveloped me in a big hug, too. His familiar Dad smell made me realize it had been forever since he'd been home.

"Good to see you girls," Dad said, unlocking our door.

"We missed you," Micki said, jumping around up and down. She almost looked happier than she had at the Intrepid museum yesterday. Wasn't it sort of sad that my little sister was so excited for him to just be home? Shouldn't your parent coming home be more of a normal, non-jumping-around type of thing? But I couldn't blame her. Since Dad had been away so much lately, this felt like a big deal to me, too. But I couldn't summon the same pure enthusiasm.

"I've missed you, too," he said as we walked inside the apartment. Dad set his suitcase down next to his favorite comfy chair. "I wasn't sure I was going to make it home today, so I told your mother not to say anything. I figured it would be a nice surprise." Dad slumped heavily into the chair. He looked tired. "Where *is* your mother?"

Had Dad already forgotten our system? "I'm sure she wrote it on the fridge board," I said. My voice sounded tight. Was I really feeling annoyed at him? He'd just gotten here. Why couldn't I be more like Micki and just be glad he was *here* for a change?

"Oh, of course!" Dad said with a laugh, slapping himself lightly on the forehead. "Sorry, I've been traveling since yesterday afternoon."

Micki was pawing through our bags from the store, ready to show Dad all the school supplies she'd picked out. I sat down on the floor and started organizing everything into a pile for me and a pile for Micki.

"Where did you fly in from?" I asked Dad, keeping my eyes on the school supplies.

"Hong Kong."

"Look, Dad, I got markers and dog stickers and—"

"Micki, hush," I said, knowing I was being a little mean. "What's Hong Kong like?" I asked Dad.

"Very big, bright, and loud," Dad said, closing his eyes. Micki perched on the arm of the chair. I wanted to ask Dad more about Hong Kong, and I especially wanted to tell him all about Four Paws, and to see if he had any business advice. But he just looked way too exhausted.

"Do you want something to drink?" I asked him instead.

"Some ice water would be great. Thanks, kid."

I checked the fridge board when I was in the kitchen and announced, "Mom went to get groceries."

Micki was chattering away at Dad, whose eyes were still closed. When I cleared my throat, holding out his glass of water, he finally opened them. "Thanks," he said again. "Listen, girls, I'm just going to grab a shower and close my eyes for a few minutes, then I'll be back to human again. You two decide where you'd like to go for dinner, okay?"

"Can we go to Motorino?" Micki asked. It was her favorite place for pizza.

Dad chuckled as he stood up. "I actually just went to the one in Hong Kong the other day."

"Oh," Micki said, deflating. "We can pick something else."

"You girls talk about it," he said, and shuffled into the master bedroom and closed the door.

"I can't believe he's back," Micki said. I noticed she'd stopped hopping up and down.

"I know," I told her. Watching her expression falling as she looked at the closed door, I thought of something to distract her. "I'm sure Dad will be napping for at least an hour, and I saw your backpack strap hanging by a few threads this week. Do you want to walk down to Marshalls? We can get you a new backpack." I still had the card Mom had given me to pay for our school supplies.

"Okay," Micki said, though she still sounded kind of glum.

I hoped Mom wouldn't mind and that I could convince her that bribing Micki with a new backpack was better than watching her disappointment grow while Dad napped.

"Look, Mom, look!" Micki said when we got home. "Kat let me get a *Descendants* backpack!"

I smiled at my sister's return to her enthusiastic self. Sometimes the little things really helped.

Mom was putting a bag of sandwiches on the counter, and she sent me an appreciative glance. Phew. "That's great, Micki. I'm glad Kat had time to take you shopping." My insides warmed knowing she was happy with me. "I picked up dinner from the deli."

"Dad said we could go out," I said, trying not to pout.

"Looks like he really needs the nap, girls," Mom said. "Maybe tomorrow."

We ate around the kitchen island, Dad's sandwich waiting for him in the fridge.

After Micki went to bed, Mom came into my room. "Hey, I know it's still pretty warm out, but do you want to make some cocoa with me?" she asked.

I nodded. We used to make cocoa at bedtime when I was little. It was kind of our thing.

I followed her out to the kitchen, and from my perch on my usual kitchen stool, I watched her pull everything out of the cabinets. Now that I was older I usually helped out with lots of chores around the house. But this was how we used to do cocoa time—Mom would make it for me.

"That was a really nice idea, taking Micki out to get a new backpack," she said, stirring the liquid in the small pot on the stove. Mom makes cocoa the old-fashioned way—she never uses the microwave.

"I'm sorry I went without asking," I said. "I know her strap was broken, but we didn't check with you first that we could get one today."

She looked up at me. "That's very mature of you, Kat. I think, today, Micki needed that, so I'm not mad."

For some reason, I felt hot tears forming in the corners of my eyes. I was glad I didn't have to explain it to Mom. She knew why I'd done it. "Thanks" was all I could say.

Mom carefully poured the cocoa into two mugs, then

added the whipped cream. There are, of course, two schools of thought on hot cocoa: the marshmallow fans and the whipped cream ones. Our family falls enthusiastically into the second group.

I accepted my mug—my favorite one, with a cartoon pug that reminded me of Meatball—and Mom sat down on the stool beside me.

"You're really growing up to be such a good big sister," she told me.

I felt the tears threaten again unexpectedly. It was nice, what she was saying to me. "Thank you," I said again, my voice sounding a little hoarse. "I'm trying."

"That's the secret to pretty much everything, kiddo. Trying." She clinked her mug against mine, and we enjoyed our chocolaty, creamy treats together.

I'd missed a text from Lucy while Mom and I were having cocoa. I saw it when I returned to my room.

Mom said she saw your dad was back. Going ok?

I didn't even really know how to answer the question. But I was grateful to Lucy for being insightful enough to ask.

Can't tell so far—he's been asleep basically since he got back. It's kind of . . . weird to have him here after so long.

Seconds later, my phone lit up with a call notification from Lucy. I answered and immediately told her, "Hey. I'm okay."

"I just wanted to check," Lucy said. "Your text sounded like maybe you weren't."

I let out a sigh as I snuggled into my blankets. "I don't even know," I admitted. "Mom and Micki and I kind of have our routine. Everything is just so different when he's here." As soon as I said the words I started to regret them—Lucy had said to me before that she wished her dad had stuck around. It had always been just her and her mom because he left when she was really little. He still sent money and cards and presents on birthdays and Christmas, but that was about it.

Although, maybe that sort of made Lucy the perfect person

to talk to. Even though my dad wasn't *gone*, he did miss a lot of things. Sometimes even birthdays and holidays.

"It's okay to talk about this stuff with me," Lucy said. "I don't mind."

"Stop reading my mind, Lucy Larrabee!" I told her.

"I'm not a mind reader, Kat Cabot," she said, laughing. "I just know you really well. We've been BFFs since fourth grade."

"I know," I said. "And thanks for checking on me. I know you're not supposed to use your phone after ten. You're not going to get in trouble?"

"Nah, Mom's down in the gym. There's a new guy she's dating." I could practically hear the eye roll in her voice, but she was mostly amused. "She's been trying to step up her game."

"I'm glad you don't mind your mom dating," I said carefully. "That she doesn't make it weird for you."

"Well, one day I'll be off being a famous actor, so I don't want her to be lonely!" Lucy said.

I had to admire Lucy's confidence that she would one day be a professional actor. Even though I felt like Four Paws was going well, I didn't feel confident that it meant I would be a successful businesswoman when I was older—*if* I decided on a business career.

"Don't I know it," I told her. "Hey, so I'll see you tomorrow to walk to school?"

"Sounds good. Night, Kat."

After I hung up, I got a text, and it was just our special emoji we'd been using since starting the business: the animal paw prints.

I sent one back and turned off the light.

11

Like Always

When Micki and I got home from school the next day, Dad was back in his favorite chair.

"Where's Mom?" I asked.

"Doing some laundry. She'll be back in a minute. Hey, kid-dos, I'm sorry about dinner last night. I guess the jet lag hit me harder than I expected."

"It's okay," I said.

Micki was getting herself some juice, not even close to jumping up and down the way she had yesterday.

"How about dinner tonight to make up for it?" Dad suggested, and I saw Micki's face brighten.

"That would be great," I said, meaning it.

Mom came in then with a big basket of laundry, and Dad told her Micki and I were on board for dinner.

"Why don't you girls do your homework and we'll leave in about an hour?" Mom asked.

I nodded and went to my room. I tried to focus on my algebra homework, but I was distracted thinking about Dad and why things still didn't feel back to normal. When the Four Paws app dinged I was relieved. I accepted the last-minute walk and hopped up.

"Where are you going?" Dad asked as I grabbed my sweater off the hook by the door.

"I have to go walk a Chihuahua."

Dad was staring blankly at me. It was very clear in that moment that he had completely forgotten my new dog-walking business. I felt a pang of relief when I saw him figure it out. "Your project for Junior FBLA," he said with a slow smile. "How's it going?"

"It's going really well," I told him, my spirits lifting. "I actually have a lot of questions I want to ask you. But I have to go walk Charlie now. I'll be back in a few minutes. This is just a do-his-business walk—not going to the park for exercise or anything."

"Okay," Dad said. "Be careful."

Charlie the Chihuahua was probably Taz's favorite dog, although their relationship wasn't as special as mine was with Meatball. Charlie lived on Taz's floor, so she was usually the one to walk him, but I knew she wouldn't mind that I'd grabbed the walk.

Taz, Lucy, and I all had the keys to Charlie's parents' apartment, like we did now with a lot of our clients. Most of the time when people need somebody to walk their dog, it's because they're not home. Taz added an option for the app where clients could indicate that we were allowed to let ourselves in.

I opened the door and saw Charlie wake up, picking up his tiny head and blinking sleepily at me. He'd been curled up in his cute little bed in the living room. He came ambling toward me, and I bent down to pet him. He really was an adorable little guy.

Charlie might be my third favorite after Meatball and Sparky, I reflected as he rolled over for me to pet his wriggling white belly.

Our walk was over almost too quickly, and when I dropped him off at home, I gave him a cookie out of their kitchen stash to spend a few more minutes with him.

When I got back downstairs, Mom, Dad, and Micki were waiting for me.

"Ready?" Mom asked, and I nodded.

Mom and Dad led the way, holding hands, without telling us where we were going. I tried to guess as we passed some of my favorite restaurants, which still had only a handful of people sitting down to dinner since it was early.

When we stopped in front of Motorino, I couldn't help but grin. Micki gave me a high five. We followed Dad inside and he led the way to a table in the back. There was a banner hanging above the table that said HAPPY BACK TO SCHOOL, KAT & MICKI!

"Oh, wow!" Micki cried, impressed.

"Sorry it's so late," Dad said. Mom leaned into the side hug he offered her, a smile creeping onto her face.

I wondered if it was Darius, Dad's overworked assistant, who'd set all this up. But the thought was still nice. I joined in everyone else's smiles. "Thanks, Dad," I said.

We sat down and ordered our usual extra-cheese pizza and a pitcher of Coke.

"How is school going so far?" Dad asked.

"Good," I said.

"Yep," Micki said.

"How is Junior FBLA?" Dad asked me as I sipped my Coke.

"Fine. We've only had one meeting." I thought back to our first meetup in Ms. Weinstein's room. She was nice and friendly. She'd never led an FBLA before, and there were only a few other kids. We'd gone around the room and shared our business ideas and given one another some tips. I didn't tell Dad that I wasn't sure how invested the other students were.

"Only one?" Dad said. "You've been back in school awhile."

"Our next meeting is tomorrow," I said as the waiter came with our steaming, cheesy pizza. Mmm. As we all dug in, I thought about how I'd been planning to ask for a dog of my own while Dad was home. I also thought of the Four Paws questions

I had for him. But somehow tonight still didn't feel like the right time to ask Dad any of these things. Maybe I would tomorrow.

But as we finished eating, Dad cleared his throat. "Girls . . . I'm afraid I have some disappointing news. I wanted to let you enjoy your pizza first."

My pizza felt suddenly heavy in my stomach.

Mom put a hand over Dad's on the table. "Dad has to go back to Hong Kong, just for a few days hopefully."

"Like, now?" I asked loudly.

"In the morning," Dad said.

"What do you mean?" Micki said.

Dad frowned. "I heard from the office before dinner. They have an emergency they need my help with."

"Tomorrow morning?" I confirmed.

"I'm sorry, girls. Hopefully it won't be for too long this time."

Micki and I didn't say anything else, and I definitely could see the guilt on Dad's face.

As I dragged my feet on the walk home, I thought of something Declan had said—that when his parents had felt guilty about him moving, he'd gotten an adorable pug puppy out of it. If I was going to be bummed about Dad never being around, maybe I could get something I wanted more than anything—a dog of my very own—out of it.

My spirits lifted as we walked inside the Burgundy. Maybe I didn't have to wait until Dad was home again to ask. I decided that I'd start working on ideas for how to ask Mom by herself. Maybe if I made a plan, just like I'd done with Four Paws, I could make it happen.

12

What Even Is My Life
Right Now?!

The next day at lunch, all anyone could talk about was the school play. The auditions for *Our Town* were later that afternoon. Lucy and Declan were auditioning, and Taz was going to sign up to do the costumes. Two other girls in our grade who sometimes sat with us—Brooke and her best friend, Misty—joined us that day, too.

I could tell Lucy was super nervous; she barely touched her lunch. I felt nervous for her, like I always did when she had an audition coming up. But I also felt sort of *not* excited about her playing Declan's wife. Why was Mr. Cornell even having us put on a play where people got *married*? We were in middle school!

The play was all Lucy had been able to talk about for more than a week. I kind of hoped that she'd calm down about it once she finally got the part—or didn't. There were a few girls in our grade who loved acting, too, so it wasn't like she would automatically get the lead. I knew that was why she was sweating the whole process so much.

"Will everyone get a part?" Brooke was asking.

"Not onstage," Misty answered. "But everyone can do something. I mean, we need understudies for all the major parts. And also we need people to sign up for stage crew. You should audition," she said to Brooke, who nodded.

I thought to myself that Brooke would definitely audition. Misty could be kind of overbearing, and Brooke usually went along with her plans.

Even though I know I also have a strong personality, Lucy pushes back (in a nice way) when she doesn't agree with me.

And, of course, Taz always gives me the real real. That's probably why the three of us are best friends; we're a good balance.

"Well, whatever part I get, I'm looking forward to it," Declan said cheerfully. "I can meet some more people, and hopefully it'll be fun. I did *The Wizard of Oz* last year at my old school, and I had a really great time. I'm still on a text thread with everyone. We have a lot of inside jokes from spending so much time doing the show."

I found myself wanting to hear about all the jokes—but that's not how inside jokes work. The bell rang for class, and I wished everyone luck as we all went our separate ways.

After my last class of the day, I showed up at Ms. Weinstein's room for FBLA. But Ms. Weinstein looked stressed. The other students and I barely got through the door before she made an announcement.

"I'm sorry, kids, I have to cancel this week," Ms. Weinstein said. "My daughter has the flu. Why don't you all get a little further with your business proposals and we can try to meet next week?"

As we all turned to leave, I gripped the straps of my backpack. It wasn't that I was so upset about missing FBLA. I cared more about Four Paws itself. But with all my other friends auditioning for the play right at that moment, my canceled meeting made my own extracurricular activity feel like a real bust.

And I blamed that feeling for what happened next: I found myself walking up to the sign-up sheet outside Mr. Cornell's room, and writing my name down for stage crew.

Stage crew?! As soon as I got home, I wondered what I had been thinking. Had I really just signed up to do theater?

Sure, I wanted to spend more time with Lucy and Taz. And Declan. But, I realized as I left the apartment to walk Biscuit, maybe it was also just plain old jealousy. I knew Lucy and Declan would bond doing the show together, and I didn't want to be left out.

Nobody likes to be left out, right? That was probably all it was.

The next day, after school, Mr. Cornell posted the cast and crew list. I gathered with the excited crowd of students to read the names. Just as Lucy had been hoping, her name was right at the top, cast as the lead character of Emily Webb. She screamed and squeezed my hand.

"Congrats!" I told her, feeling a rush of joy for my friend.

But then I felt a funny pang when I saw that Declan had gotten the part of George Gibbs—Emily's husband. Brooke would be playing George's sister, Rebecca. Misty got a big part, too—the Stage Manager. I thought it was probably an appropriate part for her. We'd started reading *Our Town* in English class, so I already knew that the Stage Manager explains everything to everybody, which is pretty much perfect for Misty.

I got the exact job I signed up for: stage crew. Thankfully, there were a few other kids on the stage crew as well, including the lighting people, the sound people, and the set-design people. Taz was the head of the costume crew, as she'd hoped to be. The understudies were listed, too: Brooke was the understudy for Lucy's part, and Mitchell Brown—who Lucy had been so afraid would be cast as George, her stage husband—was Declan's.

Once Lucy had stopped squealing, she saw my name listed

as stage crew and threw her arms around me in a huge hug. "I can't believe you signed up, but I'm so glad you did!"

"It was a last-minute decision," I said.

"I'm glad, too," Declan said, which made my cheeks flush a little.

"Me three!" said Taz, giving me a high five.

Everyone headed into the after-school meeting in Mr. Cornell's room, where he gave out the rehearsal schedule. Holding the paper, I started to worry about Four Paws. I wouldn't be able to do stage crew after all if I had to be at all these rehearsals.

I went up to Mr. Cornell, feeling a little nervous since I'd never actually talked to him before. "Um, Mr. Cornell? I'm Kat Cabot. I signed up for stage crew. And I'd really like to do it, but now that I see the schedule, if I have to be at all the rehearsals, I won't be able to—"

Mr. Cornell put up one hand. "Hi, Kat. Thank you for signing up for stage crew. We really need the help. But since there are several kids on the stage crew, you don't have to be at *all* the rehearsals. I would mostly need you the two weeks leading up to the play. Do you think you could do that?"

Whew. "I'll see if I can. Thanks, Mr. Cornell."

"Be sure to let me know ASAP if you can't," he told me.

I walked over to rejoin Lucy, Declan, and Taz. "What was that about? You weren't quitting already?" Lucy asked.

"No. I mean, not yet. It's just—Four Paws has to come first for me. We've made a commitment to our clients. Mr. Cornell said I mostly have to do the two weeks leading up to the play. But I also have a huge project for social studies. I just don't know how I can fit it all in." I put a hand to my forehead and tried to breathe. "We can barely keep up with all our Four Paws clients as it is!"

"What if you had another dog walker in the mix?" Declan asked. "To help with Four Paws?" He gave me a meaningful smile.

"Ooh, that's a great idea!" Lucy exclaimed.

I blinked at him. "Do you mean you? Declan . . . that'd be great! But you just got this big part . . ."

"Yes, but Mr. C rehearses us in groups for the first week or so. I won't have to be at all those rehearsals," Declan explained. "What if I helped out now and then you could finish your social studies project before the play really heats up?"

Declan, becoming our fourth Paw? It really did seem kind of perfect. I couldn't help but smile.

"What do you think?" I asked Taz and Lucy.

They both nodded. "Sounds awesome to me," Taz said.

I extended my hand for Declan to shake. "Deal. Welcome to Four Paws."

Declan laughed and shook back. "Deal."

I asked everyone to wait for me while I went to get Micki, who was playing on her tablet and sitting in the hall. Oof—Micki. I *really* hadn't thought everything through before jumping in to sign up for the play—if I stayed after school for rehearsals, Micki would be stuck here, too. Mom and Dad would never let her walk home alone, and Mom had to work and couldn't come and get her. I guessed I'd just have to ask Mom if it would be okay if Micki stayed and did her homework and waited for me during the two weeks leading up to *Our Town*.

When I got home and asked Mom, she surprised me by saying, "You're helping with the play? That's great!" I guess she was pleased I was doing more extracurricular activities.

"But Micki . . ." I started to remind her.

"Micki can stay after school for a few days. She can do her homework. Maybe she'll find an interest in drama, too. You never know."

"Okay. Should I tell her?"

"Let's wait until that week," Mom said, smiling conspiratorially.

"Deal," I said, for the second time in two hours.

Later that evening, I knocked on the Thompsons' door to pick up Meatball for our walk.

Dan Sr. answered. "Hi, Kat," he said. "Come on in."

I walked in and was glad that everything seemed calmer than usual. I felt bad for the Thompsons when it was chaotic in their apartment. Sometimes I thought little Meatball looked like he wanted to go somewhere calmer and quieter, too.

"How are you guys?" I asked, looking around for Meatball.

"Doing okay. How's school?"

"It's okay," I answered. Where was Meatball?

"DJ's school finally started last week. Thank goodness," he added with a laugh. I didn't join in; I'm not Dan Jr.'s biggest fan since I don't think he's super nice to Meatball, but I wouldn't ever say anything to his parents, of course.

Finally, I spotted my Meatball. And I realized why he hadn't come running when I came into the apartment. He was very focused on scratching himself.

"Hey, Meatball!" I called. He looked up, but almost seemed to frown, and kept scratching.

"What's the matter with him?" I asked Dan, who made a puzzled face.

"I don't know," Dan said. "He wasn't doing that before."

I crouched down beside him. "Hey." I grabbed his back paw, and he looked up at me, a mournful expression in his dark eyes. I could have sworn he was trying to say, *Help me, Kat!*

"He's *really* itchy," I said to Dan, but he was typing on his phone and didn't seem to hear me. I felt a surge of frustration. If only Meatball were my dog. His super itchiness wouldn't be a distraction—it would be, like, the main focus of life.

Dan looked over at me. "Did you need anything?" he asked me.

It seemed like a dismissal. I got his message. I was supposed to take Meatball for his walk, like they were paying me for.

I scooped up my itchy little Meatball in my arms. He licked my face once, and I gave him one quick kiss on his head. I carried him to the doorway and put him into his harness. "We'll be back in a little while," I said to Dan.

"Okay, thanks."

Once we were walking outside in the sunshine, Meatball stopped scratching, mostly. But then he stopped to smell the grass and then ended up plopping down to go after the itch again. I knelt down and looked him over; his belly was much pinker than usual. Maybe I could find something to soothe his skin. The pet supply store over on 81st Street would probably have something. I thought about taking Meatball back to his family's apartment while I went to the store, but the idea of sending him back there with no one, maybe, to stop him scratching . . . the skin on his poor belly was already so inflamed!

It was kind of far to carry him—I mean, Meatball did love his treats so he wasn't light. It wouldn't be like carrying Declan's tiny little Spark Pug. Of course, Declan had that handy carrier. That was it! I knew what I needed: a way to carry Meatball. The Worthingtons on the seventh floor had a dog carriage down in their basement storage that they sometimes used to walk their Yorkie-poo, Meredith. And I had the key, since I was the one who usually walked Meredith. I didn't think the Worthingtons would mind if I borrowed their dog carriage. I could ask them . . . but I knew for a fact that they were still in Palm Beach.

My heart started beating a little bit faster as Meatball and I headed back toward the Burgundy. I knew what I was doing was at least a little bit wrong. But it was for a good cause.

I'd do almost anything for my Meatball.

Marcel waved me through the door when I went into the storage area, and he didn't even blink when I walked back out pushing the stroller ahead of me, Meatball tucked safely inside.

Back out on the sidewalk, I looked down at him as we walked. The little guy really seemed to be enjoying his ride! He was sitting up and looking around. He was only scratching a little bit. We made it to the pet supply store, where every customer oohed and aahed at how cute he was in his little (borrowed) stroller.

And for Meatball's part, he was totally soaking up all the attention, his tongue hanging out to one side, only an occasional itch to remind me why we'd had to come here.

I decided to wait to put on the cream until we'd returned the stroller so none of it would get on the blanket or the pad inside.

I patted Meatball on the head and he let out a happy bark.

When we got back to the Burgundy, I was surprised to see Marcel frowning when I pushed Meatball inside the lobby.

He stepped forward and peered into the stroller. "That's not Meredith," he said, raising an eyebrow at me.

My whole body seemed to go cold in a matter of a second, and my head felt strange. I never got in trouble. Because I always followed the rules. So this was an entirely new, and completely terrible, experience. "No," I admitted. "It's Meatball."

"I know Meatball," Marcel said. "When you took the stroller out of storage, I assumed you were taking the Worthingtons' dog. Did you ask them to use the stroller for another dog?"

I thought, very briefly, of lying. But what if Marcel had already checked? And more importantly, I knew I couldn't do it. So I just shook my head.

Marcel looked at me sadly. "That's not like you, Kat," he said, and then I felt even worse. "I remembered that the Worthingtons took Meredith with them on their trip. I almost called them. And if something like this happens again, I certainly will."

"I'm so sorry!" I said, tears welling up in my eyes. "Marcel, I really didn't mean to cause a problem. I just—I thought it was the perfect solution to borrow the stroller, just for a little. I'm sorry," I repeated. "It won't happen again."

Marcel nodded. I guessed he was waiting to take the stroller back from me. He wasn't even going to trust me down in the storage area again. I understood. But it still stung. I reached down to pick up Meatball and held him close as I watched Marcel take the stroller away.

I felt awful. And now I had to go give Meatball back, so the day wasn't getting any better. I carried Meatball into the elevator. All of a sudden, I felt like crying. Even though it seemed like the crisis with my "borrowing" the Worthingtons' stroller had been sort of sidestepped, I still felt terrible. And I hadn't just put my own trustworthiness on the line; I represented all of Four Paws when I walked our customers' dogs.

I rang the doorbell at the Thompsons' and Sarah answered. "Oh, hi, Kat. Is everything okay?" she asked as she took off Meatball's harness.

I nodded. Thankfully, I'd managed not to actually cry. "When I came to get him before, Meatball was really itchy, and his stomach was all pink from scratching. So I went and got this cream. Would it be okay if we put some on him?"

"Oh, Kat, of course! Thank you for going to all that trouble," Sarah said gratefully. "I'll put it on him right now, promise. What do I owe you for the cream?"

I shook my head. "Really, it's nothing. I was just happy to help Meatball." I knew it wasn't the right business decision, but I still felt guilty about taking the stroller, and in a weird way this felt like I was trying to make up for it.

Sarah gave me a strange look, but then just nodded her head. "Okay, if you're sure. Thank you again, Kat. We'll see you after school tomorrow?"

I nodded. "Sure thing. Bye, Meatball. Oh, and bye, Sarah," I added with a wave.

Sarah waved back and closed the door.

Meatball's frowny face looked almost forlorn as the door closed. Maybe he was just picking up on my feelings. Because *forlorn* was exactly how I felt just then.

13

Way Too Many Paws

Friday was supposed to be Declan's first day on the job for Four Paws. The plan was that he and I would walk a bunch of dogs together after school, so I could show him the "ropes" as I'd done with Lucy. Since Declan already had a dog, I knew he'd be more experienced than Lucy right away, but I was happy to introduce him to the Burgundy pups.

I couldn't wait for him to get started. We had so many dogs lined up, and both Taz and Lucy were busy with rehearsals. But then Declan texted me after school to say that Mr. Cornell needed him for a rehearsal that day, too.

I checked the app with a sigh as I walked home with Micki. A bunch of our clients' dogs had to be taken out pretty much now. There was only one thing I could do: take out all the dogs at the same time myself!

I made sure Micki was set with her snack and starting her homework and then set out to pick up the dogs. I picked up Charlie the Chihuahua, Mary-Kate and Ashley the Yorkies, Meatball, and Rufus the labradoodle.

Joseph, who was on doorman shift that afternoon, gave me a slightly worried look as he opened the door for me and my five dogs. I understood his concern, but I felt confident that I could get them all outside and doing their business without any problems.

With leashes wrapped in both hands, and Rufus pulling ahead of the little dogs, I managed to cross the street over to the grass by Riverside Drive. Even with Charlie scooting in between the other dogs' legs, my little troop started to sniff around like they were supposed to. But then Charlie started sniffing Mary-Kate's backside, which made Ashley bark at him. Rufus loomed over them—he seemed only to want to make friends, but instead he tangled the leashes so much I wasn't sure how I'd get them *un*tangled. Meatball sat at my feet and gazed up with a look like, *Really??*

I reached into my pocket for my treat bag. When Rufus realized what I was doing, he started jumping toward me, so I held the treat bag over my head. Of course, that made the leash tangle even worse.

My heart started pounding fast. I needed help. I looked at the people walking by, thinking maybe someone nice with five minutes to spare might stop and help me. But how could I trust a stranger enough to hand them the leash of someone else's dog? What if they just took off with one of my little charges? It was unlikely for sure, but I couldn't rule it out. Meanwhile, Charlie kept running figure eights around the other pups in nervous excitement, and they were all starting to bark, and it was getting harder to hold them by the minute. My good boy Meatball stood calmly as Ashley put her paws up on his back. Now I was really starting to sweat.

Just then Brooke from school started crossing the street. I wanted to wave a hand, but I didn't have one to spare. So I called loudly, "Brooke!"

She came over to me. "Kat. What in the world?"

"You know how I'm doing this dog-walking business?"

Brooke let out a little laugh. "Yeah. With Taz and Lucy, right? But I guess I thought you walked them, like, one or two at a time."

I let out a small wail. "I usually do! But Taz and Lucy and Declan are all at rehearsal. I guess I got . . . overconfident."

Brooke laughed again. "It's good I was walking by," she said. "I can help you."

"Are you sure, Brooke? Don't *you* have rehearsal?"

"Nope," she said. "I didn't need to be there today, so I was just coming to sit in the park for a little bit. I love the fall weather." She smiled down at my tangle of barking pups. "Here, which one should I try to get free?"

I breathed a sigh of relief. "Okay, do you mind picking up Charlie? He's the little Chihuahua. He's the one tangling them in circles."

Brooke picked Charlie up gingerly and managed to fish his leash out of the big knot. Then she took Rufus's leash, and with them separate, I could free well-behaved Meatball and the two Yorkie siblings.

"Phew!" I sighed. Brooke cuddled Charlie against her chest. "Thank you, Brooke!" I said. "Hey, I don't suppose you'd consider . . ."

"Of course I'll help you get them back," Brooke said as she placed Charlie on the ground. Now that the fun seemed over, and we could spread them out, the dogs finally got down to their business.

"Hey, you're not interested in an after-school job, are you?" I asked. Maybe we needed a *fifth* Paw!

Brooke smiled. "Thanks for the offer, but I'm only in this neighborhood one week out of the month. I'm usually with my mom Ari. We live on the East Side, and I take the crosstown bus to get to school. My other mom, Kelly, lives over here." She nodded down the block.

"Oh, I didn't know. Well, I'm so glad you were here with Kelly today. You saved my life!"

"Glad I could help," Brooke said. She watched over the dogs while I scooped the poop of the dogs who'd gone number two.

"Is it hard?" I asked Brooke as together we gathered up the leashes and turned to head back to the Burgundy. "To only see

Kelly every three weeks? Or do you see her sometimes even when you're with Ari?"

"Not too often," Brooke said. "Kelly travels a lot for her work."

I was realizing that Brooke and I had more in common than I'd ever known. "My dad travels a lot, too," I said. "He was just home for less than two days, but before that he was gone for a month."

Brooke frowned. "That must be tough."

"Sometimes it really is." I looked down at the dogs trotting along peacefully between us. "Hey, Brooke, maybe when you're over here again we could go get some ice cream or something," I said.

Brooke perked up. "I'd like that."

"How come you look surprised?" I asked.

"I just always figured you, Lucy, and Taz didn't really need anybody else."

"I don't see how you could ever have too many friends," I told her as we crossed the street back to the Burgundy. "But . . . as it turns out . . . you can definitely have too many dogs out on a walk at one time!"

Brooke laughed along with me.

"Needed a friend to get back, huh?" Joseph asked as we walked in.

"I definitely did," I said, giving Brooke a smile.

14

Celebrity Sighting

Luce, come over for clothing emergency! Pls ☺

I sent the text and peered anxiously into my closet. Normally, I would text Taz about fashion, but she was busy preparing for her family's party. Every year at the end of September, the Topolskys threw a big party because Taz's parents both have their birthdays around then.

They reserved the rooftop of our building and everyone brought tons of food. It was always really fun. But I couldn't decide what to wear.

"What's up, Kat?" Lucy said when she arrived in my room. "What do you mean, emergency?"

I looked down at the yellow dress I'd put on. "Is this too fancy? I know it's not that kind of party, but I sort of wanted to look nice . . ."

"You'll look great no matter what," Lucy said. She wore leggings and a cute striped T-shirt. "It isn't like you to worry about clothes!"

"I know." I shrugged, looking into my closet again. I thought I knew where my extra nerves were coming from—a certain newcomer to the annual party—but I couldn't bring myself to say it aloud to Lucy. "How about this?" I asked, holding up a purple shirt. "With jeans?"

"Stay in the dress," Lucy said. "Let's go! Party's already started."

I came out of my room to find Micki waiting eagerly in the living room. But Mom was still wearing her fluffy blue robe—the one that only made an appearance when she was either sick or feeling blue herself.

"You're not going," I said. It wasn't a question. I could tell what the answer would be.

"Hi, Lucy," Mom said before turning to me with an apologetic smile. "Just not feeling up to a party today. But you girls go on ahead. Have fun for me."

"We could stay with you," I suggested.

"Yeah," Lucy said. "We could all watch a movie or something."

"You three aren't staying inside on this beautiful day. Besides, I know you look forward to this party every year."

I wondered if Mom would go to the party if Dad were here. It seemed like they both used to have a lot of fun when we all went together.

Micki ran over and gave Mom a hug. I opened the door to the fridge and pulled out the big containers of cut-up watermelon that I'd promised to bring upstairs. "Are you sure you don't want to come?" I asked Mom. "We could wait while you get ready . . ."

Mom shook her head. "Nope. I'd actually love a couple hours to myself to watch HGTV." Micki groaned and Mom smiled.

No doubt Mom knew the reaction she'd get from mentioning her favorite channel that the rest of us didn't really like.

"Okay, we'll be back later. Text me if you need anything, okay?"

Mom gave me an almost stern look. "Katherine Ann Cabot. I'm the one who will receive a text if anything is needed. Got it?"

I gave her a salute. "Yes, ma'am."

Mom smiled as she tightened the belt around her fuzzy robe. "Go have fun, you."

Lucy, Micki, and I headed into the elevator and rode up to the roof. As always, the Topolskys had decorated the rooftop to look gorgeous—there were fairy lights strung up and tables with platters of food. People mingled, eating and drinking and admiring the amazing view of the Hudson River.

Taz appeared, wearing a black top and a long flowy skirt— the kind of thing that looks cool on her, but that I could never in a million years pull off.

"You made it!" Taz said, grinning at me, Micki, and Lucy. "Here, let me take those from you, Kat. You're starting to drip."

I looked down and realized that I'd been holding the watermelon containers sideways. "Oops. Sorry."

Taz shrugged. "It'll still taste good."

"Ooh, brownies!" Micki cried, noticing the snack table.

"Mmm, brownies," Lucy echoed. "Okay if Micki and I go over there now?" she asked me.

"Sure," I said, and the two of them hurried off to check out the brownie situation.

"Hey, Kat!" someone called. My heart jumped at the familiar voice, and I glanced over to see Declan coming toward me and Taz. He looked especially cute tonight in a polo shirt and jeans. And in his arms . . . was Sparky!

"Awww, you brought your puppy!" I cried. I leaned forward to give Spark Pug a kiss on the top of her furry, soft head. But I realized that doing that brought my head super close to Declan, and I felt very self-conscious. I also felt my face start to turn pink. I was 1,000 percent sure that Taz was giving me one of her *looks*, but I didn't dare glance her way. I straightened up and tried to act casual.

"Is this a dog-friendly shindig?" Declan asked Taz.

I giggled at the word *shindig*.

"Of course," Taz told him. She gestured around the roof to show that many of the guests—residents of the building plus friends of Taz's parents and sisters—had brought along their dogs. I smiled seeing so many of our clients up here. Sadly, Meatball wasn't around because the Thompsons were visiting Sarah's parents upstate that day. But I was actually supposed to walk Meatball the next day.

"I'm really sorry I had to flake on dog walking yesterday," Declan said to me.

"Oof," I said, remembering my giant dog tangle. "It worked out, but you kind of owe me. Since you weren't there, I walked so many dogs at once that I got wrapped in a knot and had to be rescued by Brooke!"

"I do owe you one," Declan said. "Next time you have to take a dog out, let me know, and I'll be there to help and learn. Promise."

I nodded. "I'm walking Meatball tomorrow. Can you meet then?"

"Yep," Declan said, holding Sparky in place as she tried to climb onto his shoulder. "It's a date."

Don't blush! I told myself. *It's just an expression!*

"Sounds good," I replied, trying to sound professional. "And Taz can even add your name to the app. Taz, you can do that, right?" I asked my friend.

But I saw that Taz's attention had been stolen away by a strange rumble that had started through the party. Jules MacNamara from school came up and whispered something to Taz, and as I looked around I saw that they weren't the only ones whispering.

"What's going on?" I asked, glancing at Declan. To my surprise, he was staring off into the distance, frowning.

Declan let out a huge sigh. "That would be Aidan," he said.

"Who's Aidan?" I asked.

"My older brother," Declan said, his voice resigned. "This kind of thing tends to happen when he shows up."

"I didn't know you had a brother."

"Yeah. Aidan's a lot older than me. He lives in LA still, but he's out here for an audition. He's trying to follow in Mom's footsteps."

I stood on tiptoe, but I didn't see what I was looking for—a taller, older version of Declan. Then a crowd of girls parted a little and I spotted him.

Now, living in New York City, you do sometimes spot celebrities. Most of them, to me at least, look pretty much like regular people. But I have spotted one or two who seem to have some kind of aura or force field around them—like they walk around in a bubble of special air, and there's no way for them to go unnoticed. Aidan Ward was like that.

"Is he famous or something?" I asked Declan.

Declan rolled his eyes. "Or something." Sparky wriggled in Declan's arms and started nosing at Declan's side. I stroked her head and her tail wagged.

"Would I have seen him in anything? Like on TV?"

"Probably not—he's mostly done commercials and small parts on television. But he was in two videos for this band, they're called the Experience? One of the videos went viral a couple months ago, and ever since, whenever Aiden goes out in public, this is what happens." Declan gestured to the cluster of people still hovering in awe around Aidan.

"I've never heard of the Experience. What kind of music do they play?"

"Terrible music, if you ask me." I smiled at Declan's grumbly tone. He scratched Sparky under her chin and she let out a happy huff.

I looked back over at Aidan. Declan's brother was cute, but I was surprised that he didn't look too much like Declan. He was shorter than I had expected, since Declan was so tall for our age. Aidan's brown hair shone gold where it caught the sun, and it skimmed artfully over his eyes. He was wearing bright-red jeans and a white T-shirt, but somehow they fit just right, and he looked much too cool to be standing there on the roof of the Burgundy with us.

Taz turned away from her whispering with Jules and asked, "Can you believe Aidan Ward is at my party?"

"Gosh, I really can't," I said in my best fake-excited voice. But Taz seemed to be following Aidan with her eyes and didn't notice.

"Man, part of my brain melted when Jules said Aidan Ward was actually *here*! I love the Experience—and that *video*!

Wait"—Taz turned to Declan—"Aidan Ward . . . is he your *brother*?"

"Guilty," Declan said.

"Wow, you have to introduce me."

Declan gave a small sigh but then nodded. "Sure thing." He turned to me. "Want to meet the man, the myth, the legend?"

"Okay," I said. "But only because he's your brother."

Declan gave me a huge grin.

Aidan was standing by the roof's edge with a plastic cup in his hand, talking with a group of older girls. Taz's sister Sariya and her friends were among them, all entranced by whatever Aidan was saying.

Declan waved to his brother, who excused himself from the group and walked over. "Aidan, this is Taz, and this is Kat. Taz and Kat, my brother, Aidan."

"Hi there, ladies. Good of you to let me tag along with baby bro here," Aidan drawled.

"Sure thing!" Taz said.

"I heard there were some secret samosas," he said. "Would either of you know anything about that?"

"I've got you," Taz said, leading Aidan away to one of the snack tables. I spotted Micki and Lucy still taste-testing different brownies; they hadn't noticed the Aidan Ward commotion yet.

Declan and I sat on one of the cushioned benches, and Declan held Sparky on his lap.

"I really did think you were an only child," I said.

"Well, I sort of am, now that Aidan's all moved out. We're really far apart in age, obviously." He scratched Sparky behind the ears and I reached over to pat her, too, careful not to get awkwardly close to Declan. "I know it seems like he really bugs me, and he does, sometimes. But it was hard when he got his own place and moved out. I think that's actually one of the main reasons Dad got me Sparky. Speak of the little devil," Declan said as she wriggled on his lap and almost jumped out of his grasp.

"I'll take her for a bit," I offered, scooping Sparky up in my arms, happy to get some cuddle time with her. She put her paw on my leg, looking up at me with her huge black eyes. I almost melted.

"So, I get that, what you were saying about missing your brother," I told Declan.

Declan nodded, giving me an understanding look. "I'm sure you do, since your dad travels so much. But that's why it's so great how you look out for your sister."

I felt myself start to blush. "Thanks. I mean, I've actually been trying to be a better big sister lately."

"You seem pretty great already."

"Thanks," I said again, blushing even more. As if she'd heard us, Micki came running over then, with Lucy strolling behind her.

"I brought you a brownie," Micki told me, proudly handing me a paper plate.

"Thanks, sis," I said. "Do you want half?" I asked Declan.

"Sure," he said, and I broke off half and gave it to him. I took a big bite of my half. Mmm. Taz's dad always made the best brownies.

"Hey, guys," Lucy said, coming over.

"Hey, Emily," Declan told her with a teasing smile. Right. The play. I went from feeling totally happy to feeling a little bit . . . irritated. I tried to tell myself I was being silly.

"Who is that cute guy Taz is talking to?" Lucy asked me,

gesturing to one of the snack tables, where Taz and Aidan were chatting away over a platter of Taz's mom's samosas.

Declan chuckled. I couldn't tell if he was annoyed or just amused. "That's my brother, Aidan," he explained.

Lucy's eyes widened. "Omg. Aidan *Ward* is your brother! *The* Aidan Ward?"

Declan sighed. "That's the one."

Lucy's face was pink. "That's amazing! Is it okay if I go over and say hi?"

"Sure," Declan said with a shrug. "Add to his fan club."

Lucy hurried off to join Taz and Aidan. Micki, on the other hand, didn't seem to care about Aidan and plopped down on the bench beside me and Declan. She focused on cooing at Sparky and petting her.

I glanced at Declan. Was *he* jealous that Lucy clearly thought his brother was cute? And was *I* jealous because I thought Declan thought *Lucy* was cute?

Why were feelings so complicated?

Soon the party was wrapping up and people started to leave. I knew Micki, Lucy, and I would stay longer to help Taz and her family clean up, like we always did. But Aidan came over to get Declan because they had to meet up with their dad. I reluctantly handed Sparky back to Declan, and Micki waved sadly to the puppy, too.

"I'll see you tomorrow for the dog walk?" Declan called to me as he and Aidan walked off.

"Yep," I said, looking forward to it, but still feeling conflicted.

"Are you okay?" Micki asked me after Declan and Aidan had left.

"Sure," I told my sister. "But maybe . . . I need another brownie."

"Of course you do," Micki said. "I'll go pick you the best one."

15

Slytherpuff

I unlocked the Thompsons' door, and Meatball bounded across the apartment to greet me. The Thompsons were taking their kids clothes shopping that day, so they'd told me to just let myself in to feed and walk Meatball. I sat down right on the tile floor in the Thompsons' foyer while Meatball kissed my face, and I giggled and petted his ears. Then he rolled over and I scratched his belly for a good five minutes at least. Finally I got up and he followed me into the kitchen. I fixed his lunch and put the bowl on the floor. While he ate, I thought about the end of the party last night—Micki and I had helped Lucy, Taz, and Taz's family clean up, which meant we got to bring some delicious samosas and brownies home as leftovers for Mom. She seemed in better spirits, so maybe her alone time with HGTV had helped.

Meatball was done eating in under two minutes flat. Pugs are great eaters—second only to dachshunds, probably. "Do you want to go outside?" I asked him, and he wriggled around happily, trotting to the door. I slipped on his harness and he let out a joyful bark. What a sweet dog he was, always happy, even though his humans were so busy and distracted.

When we stepped off the elevator, right away I spotted Declan in the lobby. He was waiting for us—with Sparky!

"Is it okay that I brought Sparky along?" Declan asked as Sparky strained forward on her leash, barking at the sight of Meatball.

"It's perfect," I said. "At last, the two cutest pugs in the building meet!"

Meatball raced over to Sparky and started sniffing her, and Sparky barked again but sniffed Meatball right back. Their tails wagged in unison. It was too adorable. Declan and I looked at each other and started laughing.

"Looks like they're instant best friends," Declan declared.

He really was the nicest, most dog-loving boy I'd ever met.

"Let's get going," I said after the dogs had finished greeting each other. "I can show you where we usually take the dogs."

Declan nodded. "Let the Four Paws training begin!"

Marcel greeted us—he seemed to have forgiven me for the stroller incident—and opened the door for us. Declan and I thanked him, and I led the way toward Riverside Park. It was a bright, sunny day with just the right amount of cool in the weather—a nice surprise after how warm it had been last night.

As we walked, Declan and I talked about everything—the school play, Four Paws, New York City versus Los Angeles. Declan explained that there are lots of neighborhoods in LA, just like in New York, and all of them are different, practically like their own small cities.

When we got to the dog run, we let Meatball and Sparky loose. I laughed in delight, watching the two of them play together and roll around. I was glad that Meatball was being careful of the much-smaller Sparky.

While the dogs played, Declan and I sat on a bench and

I showed him how the Four Paws app worked—how he could claim a job and text with a client, and how the payment methods worked. (Taz had helpfully added Declan's name to the app already.) I also gave him the quick rundown of who the toughest dogs in the building were, and who were the easiest, and which ones needed special food or medicine. Soon Declan was all caught up on the ins and outs of Four Paws.

Finally it was time to head back, so we put Meatball and Sparky on their leashes and led them out of the park. We were about three blocks from the Burgundy when the sky turned suddenly dark, and out of nowhere it started pouring rain. We'd been ambling along slowly, but Declan scooped up Sparky and we started running.

"Hold on," I said. I knew I shouldn't make poor Meatball run so far so fast on his little legs, either. Declan seemed to realize what I was doing, and he handed me Sparky, then scooped up the bigger pug. I was perfectly capable of carrying Meatball on my own, but I still appreciated Declan being so chivalrous.

"Come on, this way!" I called, cradling Sparky against my T-shirt. I had an idea of a place to get out of the rain. I ran to the bookstore that had closed the year before, on 82nd. The big awning outside was still up. I leaned against the brick wall once I'd made it, and Declan was right behind. It was raining just about as hard as possible right now—the drops had actually kind of hurt my skin as we'd run the last bit. Declan put Meatball down, then leaned against the wall, too, breathing hard.

"Good call on this spot," he told me.

"I know the neighborhood," I told him as I wrung out my hair.

"What was this place?" he asked. There was black paper up behind the glass so it was obvious the store had closed.

"It was a used bookstore called the Author Attic. It closed last year."

"That's a bummer. It sounds cool."

"It really was. They sold coffee and hot chocolate, and the owner would make Rice Krispies Treats every Friday and give them out."

"Man, I'm sorry I missed that."

"You like to read? I mean, I guess so since you read most of *Our Town* before it even got assigned in class."

"Well, I was trying to figure out if I wanted to audition, and if so, for what part. But yeah, I do like to read."

"Who's your favorite writer?" I asked him.

"It's hard to pick, but right now I really like Shirley Jackson. She wrote *The Haunting of Hill House*? I'm kind of into creepy stories lately. What do you like?"

I was still holding Sparky and petting her head, but Meatball was starting to get jealous, I guess, because he barked twice at us. I smiled and handed the puppy back to Declan. I knelt down and scratched Meatball's ears. "Sorry, buddy," I told Meatball, then glanced back at Declan. "I guess my all-time favorite is J. K. Rowling. I mean, I'm still waiting for my Hogwarts letter."

"What house do you think you'd be in?" he asked.

I hesitated for a second, then decided to tell him. "I usually get sorted into Slytherin when I take the quizzes online."

Declan grinned. "Huh, I would not have guessed that. I would have thought you were Hufflepuff, like me."

"That is the other one I get. But since I got Slytherin on Pottermore, I felt like that test was more, like, scientific."

"Well, remember, in the books, Harry got to choose. So you

can decide your own house, at least that's what I'd say."

"That is a good way to look at it," I agreed. "Or maybe I'm just a combination. A Slytherpuff."

"Or a Hufflerin?" Declan laughed. "You're right, Slytherpuff sounds way better. I think my second choice is Ravenclaw. Would that be Huffleclaw or Ravenpuff?"

Now I was laughing. "Both of those work, but I kind of like Ravenpuff the best."

I looked out to see that the pounding rain had stopped and it was barely even drizzling anymore. I'd never been so disappointed in the weather before.

"Guess we should head back," Declan said.

"I guess so," I said, and we walked back to the Burgundy. We rode up in the elevator, and when Declan got to his floor, he thanked me for the training session and waved goodbye to me and Meatball. I watched Meatball watch Sparky trot out with Declan, and I could have sworn the sweet pug let out a small sad whimper.

And I kind of understood how Meatball felt—and not just because I was sad to say goodbye to Sparky.

16
Gryffindor Moment

"Reset for act one!" Mr. Cornell called. Before I even knew what was happening, Micki was hurrying out onstage with the cardboard stove needed for the scene.

I jumped, realizing that my little sister was doing my job faster than me. I grabbed the rack of containers labeled MILK to hustle to its spot.

There weren't very many props in *Our Town*. This made things easier for the stage crew, which was good—since I seemed to be so bad at it.

With the play less than two weeks away, I'd started attending rehearsals as Mr. Cornell had asked. Mr. Cornell had noticed Micki waiting around for me and had drafted her to help, too. And from the start, Micki had been the superior stage crew member. She was great at knowing when we needed to bring out new props, or whisk old ones away. Even the other stage crew members were impressed by her. And I had to admit, I was, too. It was nice to see my little sister come into her own (even if she sometimes made me look worse by comparison).

I settled back into my spot in the wings as the actors got in their positions to run the scene again. Micki stood in the wings, too, watching the stage raptly. There's a lot of downtime in stage crew, but you still have to watch and listen, and when it's time to jump in, you have to *jump*. It seemed like something I should be awesome at . . . but all that waiting had my mind wandering. I kept trying to sneak work on my homework, or glances at the Four Paws app, even though I knew Taz had us covered on the dog walks. (She wasn't as involved in the rehearsals this week, since the costumes were all set.)

Maybe I was more of a Ravenclaw than I'd thought. Sneaking homework definitely seemed pretty Ravenclaw.

And my other distraction? Sparky. Since Declan's dad had to work late nights this week, he brought Sparky to Declan during after-school rehearsal. Mr. Cornell wasn't exactly thrilled about it, and technically there weren't supposed to be any animals at our school. But I guess after hours, when your super-talented lead actor needs to look after his new puppy, the rules get kind of flexible. I teased Declan that he was becoming more of a Slytherpuff, since the rules *apparently* didn't apply to him.

Sparky's crate was stationed right next to me in the wings. She didn't *need* much attention—she was snoozing happily at the moment, totally not caring that she was in our school theater. But I was constantly stealing glances at her to marvel at her cuteness and make sure she was doing okay.

I refocused on the actors. Brooke was speaking her lines as Rebecca, a character I sort of related to. She complains in the play that all the outfits she has to wear to school make her look "like a sick turkey," which I totally got, and also she's good with saving money. I realized I enjoyed watching the rehearsal. Even if I wasn't as good as Micki, I was grateful I'd signed up for stage crew after all.

And okay, to be honest, it was fun to watch Declan. He'd turned out to be an amazingly good actor. Everyone else (even Lucy at times, if I was being completely honest—not that I would *ever* tell her) was often obviously reciting lines; I could hear how memorized the words were. But not Declan. When he spoke, it was as though he really were George Gibbs from 1901, as though those were his actual thoughts and feelings. Maybe Declan had inherited his talent from his mom. And maybe Aidan Ward wouldn't be the only famous Ward brother. I thought about saying that to Declan, but I had a feeling it would embarrass him.

At the end of rehearsal, Declan came over to get Sparky, and we all walked home with Lucy and Micki. Outside the Burgundy, I saw two familiar faces—Taz was just coming back from her walk with Meatball. I felt a pang of sadness that I hadn't been able to do any dog walking yet this week because of the play.

As soon as Meatball saw Sparky, he raced forward on his leash just as Sparky raced forward on hers. They met in the middle and rubbed noses.

"Oh my goodness, that's too adorable!" Taz cried.

"Yeah, they're basically best friends now," I said, crouching down to rub Meatball's ears.

"Ever since their special hangout in Riverside Park," Declan agreed, and I blushed a little, remembering how nice that day had been.

Taz, Lucy, Declan, and Micki chatted about *Our Town* while I stayed in a crouch and admired Meatball and Sparky, who were busy sniffing each other again.

"Hey, Kat, would you mind doing me a favor and dropping off Meatball upstairs with the Thompsons?" Taz asked, checking her phone. "My mom asked me to pick up some bread from Zabar's."

"Of course! No problem," I said, getting to my feet and taking Meatball's leash from Taz.

"Thanks," Taz said with a knowing smile. Taz knew me well enough to see that she was really doing *me* a favor by giving me extra time to spend with Meatball.

At dinner that night, Micki told Mom all about *Our Town* and the props, and Mom practically beamed at me. I knew she was excited that my signing up for stage crew had also led to Micki being involved in the play.

"And then Declan was saying his big monologue, and Sparky started barking from her crate, and Mr. Cornell was yelling so loud a vein popped out in his forehead!" Micki said, holding her stomach as she laughed.

"That was pretty funny," I said, spearing a green bean. "Poor Mr. Cornell. I'm glad I was there to take Sparky out of her crate and hush her."

"Well, Kat," Mom said. "Sounds like you found plenty of extracurriculars this year."

"That's true!" My zero activities had morphed into three: FBLA, Four Paws, and now stage crew. "My favorite part is that stage crew ended up having dogs in it after all!"

Mom laughed again. "Good to know you can be convinced into anything if there's a dog involved . . ."

What could I say? It was true.

Which reminded me: My plan to ask Mom for a dog had never happened. Even though I'd written down all my great reasons in my notebook, every time I imagined asking her, I knew she'd say, *Ask your father*.

But tonight, I remembered, we'd be Skyping with Dad after dinner. Now was my chance to ask—and I was going to do it.

After dinner, Mom, Micki, and I gathered around the laptop, and Dad's tired-but-smiling face appeared on-screen. I decided that I could channel my inner Gryffindor, be brave, and ask Dad the question I'd been too nervous to ask when he'd visited.

I waited until it was my turn to talk to Dad by myself. Mom and Micki went off to Micki's room and I sat on the couch, facing Dad on the laptop. He asked me about FBLA again. I told him we'd only had two meetings, but Four Paws was going well. Then I took a deep breath and just asked.

"Dad, can I get a dog?" He immediately looked surprised, so I sped into my arguments. "I've proven how responsible I am with animals by running Four Paws. I mean, I take care of, like, twenty other people's dogs. I could easily take care of my own."

The image of Dad's face froze for a few seconds, and I held my breath, waiting.

"Kat," he started, his face still frozen but his voice coming through. Then, all in a rush, the connection caught up, and his head moved back and forth a few times, super fast. But I was too nervous to laugh. "You know your mom and I are away too much for us to have a pet."

"But I can take care of the dog," I said. "That's what I'm telling you. *Other* people pay me to take care of *their* dogs. How would this be any different? Besides, I'm trustworthy. I take care of Micki, too."

"I know, kiddo, and I appreciate it, but I'm afraid getting a dog right now is out of the question."

I knew I shouldn't, but I couldn't help adding, "You and Mom being busy is really even *more* reason to get us a dog, so that Micki and I won't get lonely."

Dad frowned. "Can you put your mom back on?"

I let out a sigh of frustration and pushed the computer away from me. "Mom!" I yelled. I ignored the questioning look she gave me as she walked back to the couch. I went to my room and slammed the door, not that Dad could hear all the way from China or Berlin or wherever he was.

Micki knocked softly a few seconds later. "Kat? Can I come in?"

"Yeah," I called.

Micki opened the door. "I heard you asking Dad about a dog. And him saying no," she said sadly. "I'm sorry."

I let out another sigh and lay back against my pillows. "He didn't even listen. I run a dog-walking *business*," I said again. "How could he not understand that qualifies me to be a dog owner? I guess he just doesn't want one."

Micki sat down on the side of my bed. "He's never even here. It should be up to Mom."

I looked at her in surprise. Micki was usually the one who defended Dad.

"Yeah," I said. "I've been meaning to ask Mom. But whenever we ask for anything big, she just says, *You have to ask your father.*"

"Well, maybe we should keep working on her. It's not fair," Micki said.

I smiled at her. "Thanks, sis. I'll take all the help I can get." I picked up my phone and checked the Four Paws app, but thankfully there were no new requests. "Weren't Sparky and Meatball cute tonight?" I asked.

Micki nodded. "*Yes*. Sparky is my favorite dog ever. Kat, if we do get a dog, can we get a puppy?"

"Maybe," I said. "I'll take any dog." Although what I was *really* thinking was that I wanted a dog exactly like Meatball.

"At least you asked Dad," Micki said. "I know that was hard."

I smiled at her. When had my baby sister gotten so darn smart? "It was."

"And we'll keep working on it. In social studies we've been learning that some wars are fought in tiny steps. Ms. Larson called it a war of partition, I think."

I smiled. "I think you mean a war of *attrition*. I think we learned that in sixth grade, too."

"Well, whatever it is, I'll fight it with you," Micki said.

I reached out to give her a hug. "Thanks, Mick," I told her. "I needed that."

17

Three Terrible Words

On Sunday, I went with Micki to see an exhibit on space at the Museum of Natural History, so I hadn't checked my phone in almost an hour. When we were leaving the museum, I saw that I had SIXTEEN missed calls from Lucy and five missed calls from Taz. There was also a long stream of texts. My heart dropped. Something had to be wrong.

I clicked on the texts, and my eyes went immediately to three terrible words:

CHARLIE IS LOST

My stomach sank. I knew Lucy meant Charlie the Chihuahua, from the tenth floor.

I scrolled frantically through the rest of the texts, but none of them contained the words I was looking for, that Charlie was *found*.

Micki took one look at my face and asked, "What's wrong, Kat? It's not Mom or Dad?"

"No, no. But something did happen," I said. "Lucy was walking one of our clients' dogs, and she says he's lost. We have to go help find him—right now!"

"Of course!" Micki said, already pulling me down the museum steps.

I raced to keep up with her. I was slower to start running because I was still in a state of shock. How could Charlie have gotten loose?

I called Taz as Micki and I raced down the street toward home. "I'm already on it," Taz said as soon as she answered. "Just meet us in the lobby, okay? I'm trying to organize a plan."

"Thanks, Taz," I said, feeling a tiny bit of relief. Taz was good in a crisis.

Who else could help? I thought about Declan. I wanted to call him but Micki was running so fast I had to work to keep up with her. I decided to call him as soon as we got to the Burgundy.

But when we raced into the lobby, he was already there.

I didn't even think about it—I ran up to him and threw my arms around him. It seemed like the most natural thing in the world.

"It's gonna be okay," Declan assured me, hugging me back.

He let me go, and Taz stepped forward, her face tight. "Hey, Kat. Glad you got here so fast. I started trying to coordinate everything, but . . ."

"I'm sure you're doing a great job. Just tell me what happened, though! How could Charlie have gotten loose?"

"We don't have time for that now," Taz said, and I was surprised that she sounded kind of stern when she said it, like a teacher. "What you need to know is that Charlie got loose near 86th Street and Amsterdam. I checked our records—he is chipped, but no collar. My parents and two of my sisters are already over there looking, and we can divide up the rest of the neighborhood and head out. Do we have a picture of Charlie?"

I started to shake my head, but then I remembered that I'd taken one when I was walking him a couple of weeks before. "Wait." I felt like my fingers were coated in butter or something since it took me three tries to unlock my phone, and then it seemed to take forever to scroll through my pictures, but I found it. "Here!" I showed Taz the photo I'd snapped of Charlie.

"Okay, good. I think you should go to that FedEx place on Broadway and get some flyers printed up. Is your mom home?"

I frowned. "No." *Of course not* was what I was really thinking. My heart was beating so fast, and I felt sweaty, and sick. I really wanted my mom.

"My dad's gonna come to help us look," Declan said. "He was just a few blocks away; he should be here soon."

"Great. Anybody else we can think of?" Taz asked.

I shook my head. Almost everyone else I could think of in the building was a Four Paws client. If they found out about this . . .

The thought of clients reminded me that we still had other dogs in the building that needed to be walked. I pulled up the schedule on the app and let out a sigh of relief. It was a light day, with only Meatball on the books.

Marcel noticed Taz, Declan, Micki, and me standing in a huddle, and he walked up to us. "Is something wrong, kids?" he asked.

"We've got a lost dog," Taz said.

I swear Marcel looked at me first when Taz said that. I guess I couldn't really complain, since I'd already shown him my irresponsible side with the stroller incident. But I still had to push down the impulse to tell him that it wasn't me.

"Where did he go missing?" Marcel asked.

Taz told him and Marcel said, "My shift's nearly over, and Joseph's already here for his. I'll head over to Amsterdam and help out with the search. Which dog is this?"

"Charlie the Chihuahua from the tenth floor," I answered.

"Has anyone called the Porters? I'm assuming they're not home yet."

Oh my goodness, I couldn't believe I hadn't thought to ask that question yet! But my brain felt so confused and muddled, it was hard to think at all. And maybe a little part of me hoped we could fix all this without them having to know.

But Taz was nodding. "I have, and I left a message to call me back, but no answer yet."

Here was Taz being good in a crisis again—she'd already called! "Where's Lucy?" I asked, realizing I hadn't seen her yet.

Just then, the door to the small bathroom in the lobby opened, and Lucy walked out. She was paler than I'd ever seen her, and I could tell right away she'd thrown up.

"You okay, Luce?" Taz asked. Lucy shook her head.

I opened my mouth to ask Lucy how she could have lost Charlie, but Taz gave me a look that stopped me. I shut my mouth. Lucy took one look at me and burst into tears.

Declan, standing near her, patted her back, and she sobbed louder and threw herself into his arms. He met my eyes over her head and sort of shrugged, but he didn't let go of her.

Taz turned to me. "Okay, you head out to get the flyers made. I'll divide up the search areas and we'll get started. I'll call you if I hear back from the Porters."

"Or if you find him," I said, although I didn't feel very hopeful.

How were we going to find one tiny Chihuahua in this vast city? And since he was an adorable dog, who was to say that someone wouldn't just scoop him up and take him for their own? Charlie was also a really trusting dog. He'd probably go along with a stranger.

Micki had been silent and wide-eyed up until now, but then she spoke up, asking, "Can I go with Taz and Declan and Lucy and help them look for Charlie?"

I shook my head. "You should come with me, Micki."

Mom and Dad didn't let Micki walk to school by herself yet. I couldn't let her go off looking for a lost dog. A lost dog was one thing, but I couldn't deal with a lost sister, too.

Micki nodded.

"Hey," I said, checking the app again. "Can someone walk Meatball in the next hour or so?"

"I'll do it now," Declan said, and I handed him the Thompsons' key with a grateful look.

Lucy continued to sob, now sitting on a bench in the lobby. I waved a resigned goodbye to her and Taz.

"I hope they find him," Micki said as we speed-walked toward the FedEx place on Broadway.

"Me too," I said, gripping her hand tight. Looking around the city streets, I felt different than I ever had before. The crowd seemed menacing, somehow. Like anyone we passed could have taken Charlie.

"Hey, Mick—do me a favor?" I said. "Can you keep an eye low to the ground, for Charlie, while we walk? Just in case? And I'll make sure we don't crash into anybody."

"Good idea," Micki said.

Please, please, please just let us find Charlie. My stomach clenched into new knots, and I wondered again: *How* had this happened? I mean, Lucy *had* been distracted with the play. And I remembered how she hadn't been totally on her game during our training session with Meatball. Had she simply let go of Charlie's leash? Or had something else happened?

When we got to the FedEx place, there were five people ahead of us in line. Micki and I exchanged desperate glances as we waited and waited. But then Micki started crying, loudly, about "her" lost dog and the time we were wasting, and all but one guy let us go ahead of them, and then the rest of the people shamed the one guy until he stepped aside, too.

Maybe Micki was as talented an actor as Declan.

"We need to get a flyer made and printed ASAP," I told the woman at the counter. "I have one picture, and I have the number right here." I scrolled through my phone to find the Porters' number. The woman gave me a strange look that I had to look up a number for supposedly my own lost dog, but then Micki let out a fresh howl, and the woman just shrugged and typed up the flyer for us. I sent the picture to the email address she gave me, and about fifteen minutes later, poof, we had a stack of 250 flyers, still warm from the copier.

I looked down at the picture I'd taken of Charlie. He was sitting on a bench in Riverside Park, with his little head cocked like he was thinking about the answer to a question. I felt a huge tug at my heart. Poor Charlie!

We also bought a few rolls of tape to start putting the flyers up right away. I'd been texting with Taz, and I knew that they hadn't found Charlie yet. My stomach hurt. I'd mostly stopped worrying about what this meant for the future of Four Paws, and started just thinking about Charlie alone, outside—lost.

I texted again to say we had the flyers, and Taz told me where she was so that we could bring a bunch of them to her. On the way to meet Taz, Micki and I put some flyers up on lampposts and the store windows that allowed us to do so. Micki had been a real lifesaver back at the mail place—saving us who knows how much time with her spontaneous crying. And after the first flyer, we got a rhythm down: Micki would hold the flyer, I'd tape, and we'd move on. Our sister mojo was really strong. I just wished it wasn't such a sad occasion that was bringing it on.

We met back up with Taz on the corner of 84th Street and Riverside. She'd set up a kind of command center there with Lara Willis, a girl who was a little older than us and lived in the Burgundy. Lara was stationed there with a notebook, and people were checking in with her.

Taz took a roll of tape and some flyers. "Someone thought they saw Charlie a few blocks over, but it was a false alarm. Declan's dad is working the lobby of the Burgundy, talking to all the residents who come in. I think maybe you should bring him a stack of these," Taz said, holding up one of the flyers.

"You're really, really good in an emergency," I told her.

"Thanks."

"Where's Lucy?" I asked. I was worried about my best friend, even if I also felt angry at her for getting us into this awful situation.

But I knew how I would feel if I had been the one to lose Charlie. I was still kind of upset with myself for the stroller incident from the other week. And this was so much worse. Even if we found him in five minutes, it was still a big thing to lose a dog. For our clients, their dogs were family. I wondered fleetingly if Declan was still helping, and if so, if Sparky was alone. I guessed she'd be okay in her crate in the apartment. Poor Declan had to be thinking what it would be like for him if he lost *her*.

"Lucy's out looking," Taz said. "I sent Declan with her. He seemed to be the one who was calming her down the most. I tried to send her home, but . . ."

I shook my head. "I just can't believe Lucy actually *lost* a dog," I burst out. "I know she's a little disorganized and scattered, but to be so tuned out you let someone else's dog get away from you . . . I'm just . . . it's just really a big mess," I finished.

Then my phone buzzed and it was Mom calling me. I explained to her what was happening. "I'll be there as soon as

I can. I'll help you look," she said, and for a moment it seemed like everything would be all right because my mom was coming.

Mom came, and so did a few other friends from school who Taz had texted, like Misty and Brooke. Brooke gave me a hug when she saw me, and I thought back to the day she'd rescued me when I'd tried to walk five dogs. *See, you mess up, too*, a little voice in my head reminded me. But then in the next second I was thinking that all five of those dogs had made it home just fine.

As the night wore on, with no sign of Charlie, we all started to realize that we probably weren't going to find him—not right away, anyway.

The Porters, Charlie's mom and dad, had been out of town for a wedding, but they texted Taz that they were flying back.

I couldn't even imagine what they must have been feeling as they packed up their things and told everyone that they had to leave, that their dog had gotten lost.

Lost. It was such a terrible word. Maybe the worst one I'd ever heard.

* * *

A little after ten o'clock, the whole search team called it a night—it was time for everyone to get some sleep.

Micki, Mom, and I walked into our apartment, and I headed for my room. I felt tired in a way I couldn't ever remember feeling before. But even though I was tired, down to my bones, I lay awake in the dark and imagined I heard little Charlie whimpering out there somewhere.

Please, let us find him, I thought. *And please let my friend Lucy be okay, too.*

Because I would have bet just about anything that she wasn't sleeping, either.

I sent Lucy a 🐾 text, but she didn't write back.

18

Just as Much

Lucy's mom let her stay home from school on Monday to look for Charlie. Of course the Porters were looking, too, now that they were back. I was on edge all day, sneaking looks at my phone between classes to see if there were any updates, but there were none.

Mr. Cornell canceled the *Our Town* rehearsal when he found out that our Emily was absent. Some of the cast, though, stayed after to rehearse their lines themselves—Declan, Brooke, and Misty among them. Taz went straight to meet Lucy and her mom in Central Park, where the search party for Charlie had gathered now. But Micki was hungry and wanted to stop at home for a snack first, so we walked back to the Burgundy together.

I saw that the Porters had made a new flyer with a better picture and it was all over the neighborhood. The new flyers also boasted that there was a five-hundred-dollar reward.

"I wonder if the reward will help?" Micki's question broke into my thoughts.

"I hope so," I told her.

Mom was home when we got upstairs. "You're here," I said, surprised.

"I know you wanted to help look for Charlie this afternoon, so I canceled my meeting. I thought I'd help, too." I stepped closer to her and gave her a big hug, which Micki then joined. It felt good to be together at a time like this. I wondered where Dad was right now.

Mom said to run and change out of our school clothes, and that she'd make us both a protein-filled snack so we'd have lots of energy for the search. We raced back to our rooms, and I texted Taz to ask exactly where she and Lucy were.

She didn't text back until after Mom, Micki, and I were in the elevator.

76th @ the park—come now someone thinks they spotted him!!!!

I read the text to Mom and Micki, and they both gasped. "Come on, elevator, go faster," Micki said.

Mom laughed. "Oh, I hope it's true. I feel so bad for Tom and Ciera," she said of the Porters. "You know, they've only been married for about a year. And Charlie was—is—like their baby."

I looked down at my sneakers. "I know it's the wrong time to say this," I said. "But I still want a dog."

Mom frowned. "I know you do, Kat. Your father told me you asked again. But you heard him . . ."

"He's never *here*," Micki cut in. "It should be up to *you*."

Mom seemed to really hear this remark, so I didn't add anything, just gave my little sister a grateful smile. "I'll think about it," Mom finally said as the elevator doors slid open. "But for now, let's find Charlie!"

I was prepared to walk, but Mom spotted a cab headed south and hailed it. The cab stopped right away, and we all piled inside.

The driver looked surprised when Mom told him we were only going ten blocks south. Mom rooted in her bag for cash and had it ready to hand to him the moment the cab stopped.

We got out of the cab, and I spotted Taz waving to us on the corner of 76th Street in front of Central Park.

"We *just* heard from a jogger in the park who thinks he saw something that could have been Charlie!" she called. "So now everyone is looking around this part of the park. Just be sure to call or text me if you think you see anything—or if you get any more tips. This could be it!"

"Great!" Mom said.

I felt a cautious rush of hope. Central Park is huge—it stretches all the way from 59th Street to 110th Street. But the fact that someone had *just* seen a dog that looked like Charlie in the area around 76th Street meant that—maybe—the little pup hadn't gone too far.

I pictured being the one to find Charlie. And boom—at that moment I had an idea. I remembered the morning I had helped find Meatball, and suddenly I knew what I needed to do. I glanced around. There were no stores along Central Park West. But I knew there was a bodega over on Columbus Avenue, one avenue away. They sold sandwiches, and I could only hope that some of those sandwiches were made with chicken. Charlie really, really loved chicken.

Quickly, I explained my plan to Mom and Micki, and soon the three of us were racing over to Columbus Avenue and the bodega on the corner.

We stepped inside and I looked around frantically. Luckily the place wasn't crowded, so I wouldn't need Micki to put on one of her performances and clear the line. I spotted what I was looking for: a tray of grilled chicken tenders.

"Can I have a lot—maybe a pound?—of those tenders?" I asked the man behind the counter.

He nodded and started to wrap them up nicely. "Can you just throw them into a bag?" I asked. "I'm in a hurry. They're to help find a lost dog. I mean, no offense, they look delicious. I'd like to come back and try them myself once we find him."

The man laughed. "No offense taken. Is this for the lost

Chihuahua?" I nodded. "I've seen the flyers. These are on the house, as long as you do come back and try them later. And give me an update on the dog?"

I nodded gratefully. "Thank you so much! You're like a New York miracle."

The man laughed. "No big," he said, handing over the chicken. "Good luck!"

"That man was so nice," Mom remarked as we all rushed out of the store. I nodded; it felt good to see the neighborhood come together for the sake of Charlie.

Mom, Micki, and I rushed back to the park to hand out chicken to all the searchers. I only hoped my plan would work.

As we entered the park, I spotted Lucy and her mom walking along one of the paths. Lucy still looked pale and upset, and there were dark circles under her eyes.

"Luce!" I called, running over and holding up the bag of grilled chicken tenders. "I have something."

Lucy stopped moving when she heard my voice. "Hey, Kat. I'm—I'm really sorry about this," Lucy said. "About . . . losing Charlie. I realize I didn't say it yesterday."

"Lucy's been devastated," her mom said, putting her hand on Lucy's shoulder.

I shook my head. "Let's not worry about any of that now. Here, I got some of Charlie's favorite: chicken. I thought if he's anywhere hiding in the trees or bushes we could use the smell to lure him out."

"That's such a great idea," Lucy's mom said. Lucy took the chicken from me without saying anything else. We all split up and started circling the edge of the park, calling Charlie's name and holding pieces of grilled chicken in our hands.

Some people walking through the park stopped to ask us if we were looking for a lost pet. A few stayed to help for a little while; most wished us luck in finding him and went on their way. No one complained about us yelling "Charlie" over and over.

I kept walking along the edge of the park, my hand full of chicken, tree branches sharp against my skin. One even cut into my cheek, and it began to sting. But I couldn't stop. We *had* to find Charlie.

Suddenly I thought I saw a flash of brown fur among some

bushes up ahead, and I called out to Lucy, who was walking several steps in front of me.

"If it was him, he's headed your way," I said.

I knew I might have just spotted a possum or even a remarkably large rat, but what if it *had* been Charlie?

Lucy nodded and hurried into the bushes. As soon as I heard her whoop of joy, I knew she'd found Charlie. We all came running: the Porters, Mom, Micki, Lucy's mom, Taz and her parents and one of her sisters—and there was Declan, who I didn't even know had made it back to look, too.

We all surrounded Lucy, who was holding tight to Charlie. The poor little guy was shaking but otherwise seemed okay. When Mr. and Mrs. Porter rushed over to him, Charlie started crying loudly, a high-pitched keening sound that would have been terrible except that it meant that he was being reunited with his parents.

After she handed Charlie to the Porters, Lucy sat down on the grass, right where she'd been standing, like her legs had given out from under her. She put her head in her hands, and I knew that she was crying. Hesitantly, I walked over to her and sat beside her. I put my hand on her shoulder, but she didn't look up.

Lucy's mom pulled her up a few moments later and led her away, as though she were much younger.

"That was a great idea, getting the chicken," Declan said. I started a little; I hadn't realized he had come up to stand beside me. "I think Charlie smelled it and that's why he came out."

"Thank you," I told him, standing up. "I'm just glad we found him." I saw that the Porters were already walking toward the park exit, taking Charlie home.

Mom was pretending to show Micki something so I could finish talking to Declan. I had to smile at that.

"And thanks for coming back out to help," I said to Declan. "It was really nice of you."

"Well, Misty basically begged me to stay and rehearse with her, and since she has such a big part, I felt like I should stay for a little while. But I'm really glad I could be here to see Charlie get found." Declan smiled. "Now, I have a puppy of my own at home who needs some dinner and a walk."

I froze. I'd been so focused on the search for Charlie that I hadn't even looked at today's schedule for Four Paws. I pulled out my phone and quickly scanned the calendar. We were only late for one of our clients—Kekáki—and then Meatball also needed to be walked, but not until a little later.

"Do you need me to take one of the walks?" Declan asked, pulling up the Four Paws app on his phone, too.

I shook my head. As the president of Four Paws, I felt it was my responsibility to explain to the clients why we were late— even if that meant admitting what had happened with Charlie. My stomach twisted. I could only hope Four Paws wouldn't suffer as a result.

As soon as I got back to the Burgundy, I knocked on Mrs. Galanis's door to pick up Kekáki.

"Hi," I said. "I'm sorry to be late walking Kekáki. Unavoidable issue today, but I promise it won't happen again."

Mrs. Galanis frowned. "I heard about your 'unavoidable issue,'" she told me. "I think you should be honest with people that you kids lost someone's dog."

My heart sank. "I wasn't trying to be dishonest, Mrs.

Galanis, I swear. It . . . it just happened yesterday, so we've been spending all our energy on finding him. I've been trying to get everything back on track."

Mrs. Galanis folded her arms across her chest. "Well, I can't say that I feel comfortable letting you girls take out Kekáki, not under these circumstances. You can take us off your list."

She shut the door before I even knew what had happened.

I felt sick. Mrs. Galanis had been sort of cold and awful and hadn't even let me explain, but she wasn't actually wrong—we *had* lost one of our dogs, for more than twenty-four hours. It was only luck (and some chicken tenders) that had brought him home. If I were a grown-up who lived in the Burgundy, and I had a dog, would *I* let the Four Paws members walk my pup after what had just happened?

My heart sank even further when I thought about the next door I had to knock on: Meatball's.

What if the Thompsons said the same thing to me as Mrs. Galanis had? What if I never got the chance to spend any time at all with Meatball? This was the worst feeling yet.

I got in the elevator, thoughts racing. Should I straight-out tell the Thompsons what had happened? Mrs. Galanis seemed to be mad not just because we'd lost Charlie, but because I hadn't told her about it.

Or should I wait until things at the building died down a little before bringing it up to the Thompsons? Unlike Mrs. Galanis, who was always home, Sarah and Dan were always running around. Maybe they didn't even know anything about what had happened, and then I'd be foolish to bring it up—opening a can of worms that I didn't need to open.

Oh, what to do?

The elevator doors opened. Decision time.

I knocked on the Thompsons' door. When Sarah answered, I said in a rush, "Hi, Sarah. I have to tell you something. We were looking for a dog that got away from one of us yesterday, but we found him."

"Oh no!" Sarah said. "What happened?"

A tiny voice inside my head said, *See, I told you they wouldn't know anything about it!*

But the truth was out now. I couldn't go back. Besides, honesty was always the best policy.

But I realized that I still didn't actually know all the details of what had happened with Charlie. Taz had stopped me from asking Lucy yesterday. Now that Charlie was back home safe, I resolved that I was going to hear the rest of the story.

"He just got away on his walk and ran off," I said. "But we made flyers right away, we all organized a search, and we found him."

Sarah put a hand to her chest. "That's awful! The dog getting out, I mean, of course. It's so wonderful you kids all worked together and found him. So glad that story has a happy ending." Sarah was already taking Meatball's harness off the hook and handing it to me. "He's just eating dinner, as you could probably guess since he didn't come running at the sound of your voice like usual," Sarah added with a smile.

I felt shaky with relief. This interaction was very different from the one I'd had with Mrs. Galanis. Was it because I'd told the truth right away? Or because Sarah and Mrs. Galanis were just such different people? I wondered if I'd ever know.

"Meatball!" Sarah called, and he came ambling out of the kitchen. When he spotted me, he put on the speed and barreled toward me, tiny corkscrew tail going wild.

"Hey, boy," I said, a sudden lump forming in my throat at seeing him. All this time with Charlie, I'd been imagining what it would feel like for me if Meatball had gotten lost. Even though he wasn't really my dog, I loved him just as much as if he were.

"Come on, boy, it's time for a walk," I told him. But he rolled over completely onto his back, all four paws waving in the air and his tongue lolling out. He refused to budge until I knelt down and scratched his belly.

I looked up and realized Sarah was watching us. "He only does that with you, you know," she said. I tried not to look surprised. It seemed like pretty regular doggo behavior to me.

I waved goodbye to Sarah and led Meatball down the hall. Thank goodness I could still be his dog walker.

While I walked, I texted Lucy to check on her, but she still didn't send anything back. Had her mom gotten mad about the lost dog and taken her phone?

I kept Meatball out as long as I thought I reasonably could, then walked home in the almost-dark. It was getting dark a little bit earlier each day. Before I knew it, winter would be here.

For some reason, thinking about the winter and snow and

the holidays made me feel sad. Maybe because everything had been so stressful and confusing with Dad, maybe because my best friend wouldn't or couldn't text me back, or maybe just because of all of it.

When I got back home, I knocked on Micki's bedroom door. She opened it, looking surprised. It was nice in her room, with only one small lamp on and all the stars and planet stickers on her ceiling glowing softly. "Can I hang out in here?" I asked her.

Micki blinked. "Course. Let me make some space." She cleared a pile of books and stuffed animals from one side of her bed and I lay down on my back, gazing up at her stars.

Micki lay down beside me. "I'm so glad we found Charlie," she said.

"Me too."

"Maybe we can use the fact that you found him as, like, evidence. With Mom and Dad. For getting our own dog."

I noticed she said *our* dog, but I didn't mind. "Well, *Lucy* found Charlie."

"But it was your genius idea, with the chicken," Micki said, and leaned her head on my shoulder.

"Thanks for saying so. Maybe it did help," I told her.

"Of course it did!"

A few minutes passed, then Micki said, "Kat?"

"Yeah?"

"I'm really glad I'm doing stage crew with you."

I felt a warm feeling go through me, pretty much the exact opposite of the horrible cold feeling I'd felt at Mrs. Galanis's door. "Me too, sis," I said. "Me too."

But then my phone dinged. I sat up and checked the Four Paws app. It was a direct message from Charlotte, Mary-Kate and Ashley's owner.

Hi, Kat. This is to let you know we won't be requiring the services of Four Paws anymore.

19

Emergency Meeting

Things only got worse from there. By the next morning, Four Paws had lost *three* more clients. I felt awful.

Micki and I waited in the lobby for Lucy and Taz to walk to school. I felt bleary-eyed from lack of sleep. Declan had texted that he'd gone in early to work on his lines with Mr. Cornell. Taz soon joined us, but Lucy didn't text back, and finally it got too late, so three of us headed off.

"Lucy hasn't responded to any of my texts since Sunday," I said to Taz. I frowned. Saying it out loud made me realize just how bad it felt that my best friend was ignoring me. It was almost like she was mad at me, except that I hadn't been the one to do anything wrong!

"Give her a break," Taz said. "She's still really upset about losing Charlie."

"Is she even coming to school today? The play's this Saturday. If she misses another rehearsal . . ."

"Mr. C is going to lose it!" Micki finished for me.

I sighed. "Listen," I told Taz. "We need to have an emergency Four Paws meeting today, after rehearsal. We've lost five clients already. We need to figure out a plan to handle the fallout from Lucy losing Charlie."

Taz turned to me as we walked. "Kat, just the other day you were saying you were overwhelmed with too many dogs to walk. Isn't losing five just sort of solving that problem?"

I felt a surge of frustration. "Taz, the only reason the schedule has been tight last week and this week is because all the Four Paws members are involved in the play. But after Saturday, that'll be over. And then what about Four Paws? What if we keep losing clients?"

"I don't know," Taz said. "I guess we can discuss everything at the meeting."

For some reason it seemed like she was on Lucy's side in all this, and it felt massively unfair. It was *Lucy* who had messed up and put us in this position.

I kept waiting for Lucy to show up in school all morning, but in second period, I heard someone say she was absent.

It felt very strange that someone other than me was telling the teacher that my best friend was absent. What was going on? Was Lucy still so upset about losing Charlie that she couldn't come to school? What about the play?

I thought about sending her another text at lunch, but then I saw on my phone I'd already sent four that she hadn't answered. It was obviously *Lucy's* turn to respond to me.

But I did go ahead and send out the group text about the emergency meeting to all four Paws. The usual way we responded that we were in for something was to send a thumbs-up. Taz sent one right away. Declan wrote back that his mom was in town, so he couldn't make it, but to go ahead without him.

A few minutes later Lucy sent her own thumbs-up. With the original three Paws in attendance, the emergency meeting was on.

First, though, came rehearsal. It was easy to see that Mr. Cornell was *not* happy that Lucy was missing another rehearsal. Brooke was filling in for her as Emily, but she didn't really know any of the lines, or where to stand or move (which I had learned was called *blocking*). I felt bad for her. Even though she'd been named the understudy, I'm sure Brooke hadn't thought that she would actually need to play the part of Emily.

Sparky was at rehearsal today, and I was watching her in the wings, as usual. She seemed a little uncomfortable in her crate, so I took her out to let her stretch after a whole day inside. I didn't just leave her loose, obviously—I tied her leash to what *looked* like a big, heavy metal cart. But when Micki asked me to help her find a prop, I turned my back on Sparky for a moment . . . and then she took off toward Declan onstage. My knot had held just fine, but apparently the cart wasn't that heavy, since when Sparky started running she dragged the cart along with her. The cart's wheels made a horrible squeaking sound, and then Sparky started barking. She didn't actually get too far—she got spooked by the cart and eventually was just hopping around—but by that point everyone onstage had dissolved into a fit of hysterical laughing. Declan, Micki, and I all rushed to Sparky, which scared her more, but Declan managed to scoop her up in his arms to settle her down.

"Sorry, Mr. C!" I called, my cheeks pink with embarrassment.

Mr. Cornell let us go early, saying it was to "try to save what's left of my sanity."

I was torn between laughter at Sparky's thankfully minor disaster and true worry about the rehearsals. We had started so strong, but with Lucy absent, the play didn't feel right. Hopefully the whole thing would come together by Saturday. And then, of course, I'd failed at my dog-sitting duty. I frowned at that.

"I'm sorry, Declan," I told him as we walked out. "I only turned my back for a minute."

"It's totally okay, Kat," he said, giving Sparky's head a pat. "It's not fair to ask you to do your stage crew job and look after Sparky. I'll see if Dad can stay with her tomorrow."

*　　*　　*

At home, I decided that since the emergency meeting was about something so upsetting, I would at least make the snacks good. Micki helped me bake some brownies, and when Mom saw what we were doing, she revealed that she'd been keeping the ingredients for Rice Krispies Treats hidden in the back of the cabinet. So she made those for us, too.

Taz showed up first. Mom had set up the brownies, the Rice Krispies Treats, some chips, and juice on our kitchen island, and Taz was delighted. I heard another knock and opened the door to find Lucy.

"Hey, why'd you knock?" I asked. "You could have just come in."

Lucy shrugged. "Sorry." She walked inside like everything was normal. But even though I wanted to believe that it was, I could still *feel* that something was off.

"Check out this spread," Taz said, piling her plate high with snacks. Lucy grabbed a plate and added a brownie and some chips.

"When you guys are ready, we can head to my room and

start the meeting," I said. "I know it's later than we usually meet and we all have homework."

I grabbed two Rice Krispies Treats for myself—they are totally my Kryptonite—and led my friends back to my room. Everyone sat in their usual places, and I opened up my meeting notebook.

I cleared my throat, feeling strangely nervous. "So of course, the first thing we have to talk about is what we're going to do next." When nobody said anything, or even crunched a chip, for several long seconds, I went on. "Because Mrs. Galanis, Charlotte Willis, Mr. and Mrs. Waters, Mina Boscowitz, and Mr. Dana all fired us yesterday."

When *still* no one said anything, I continued. "I think the first thing we need to do is officially inform the clients we still have about what happened with Charlie."

"It's all over the building," Taz said.

"I know," I said, and let out a small sigh. "But I think Mrs. Galanis was also partially mad that I didn't explain what had happened right away. When I got to her apartment, it was right after we'd found Charlie, and I was all flustered and didn't have an explanation prepared or anything. I decided to take a different tack when I went to the next apartment, which was the Thompsons. I told Sarah right away."

"How did she react?" Taz asked.

"She said she was just glad that we'd found Charlie."

"What did you tell her?" Lucy spoke for the first time.

"What?"

"What did you tell her?" she repeated. Her voice sounded oddly flat. "Mrs. Thompson?"

"I told her the truth. That one of our dogs had gotten loose, and that we organized up and found him."

"I see. You didn't tell her that the dog walker who lost him was disorganized and scattered? That she made a really big mess for everyone?"

My whole body went cold.

Suddenly I understood just why Lucy had been so frosty to me for the past few days.

"I heard you," Lucy said, confirming what I already knew. "When we were all out looking that first night, I *heard* what you said to Taz about me. My *best friend* . . ."

Lucy's voice broke on the last two words, and at the exact same time, my heart broke.

But I also started to feel really hot all over. I realized I was also really, really mad.

The voice that had been echoing in my head for the last forty-eight hours repeated, but it was *loud* this time.

I didn't do anything wrong!

Why should I have to be the one to feel bad here?

"I'm really sorry I said that," I told Lucy. "But, Lucy, you *did* mess up. You put Charlie in danger. You put the *business* in danger."

Lucy didn't meet my eyes or say anything back.

"Well, this is awkward," Taz said after a long—in fact, truly awkward—silence.

"I'm sorry," Lucy finally said. "It was an accident."

"What *did* happen with Charlie?" I asked.

Lucy looked down at the floor and spoke in a rush. "I decided to take a different route with him, because there was some construction blocking the way to Riverside Park. Charlie noticed another dog up ahead, and before I knew it, he'd shot forward and I dropped the leash. I leaned over to pick it up, and by the time I looked up again, Charlie was racing down the block. I chased him, but he was going way too fast and there were too many people between us. I ran as fast as I could—but—but then I lost sight of him." Lucy put her face in her hands. "He was just . . . *gone.*"

Another long, terrible silence filled the room.

"I'm sorry," Lucy said again. "I haven't been able to sleep since it happened. That's why I stayed home from school again today, so I could sleep in a little."

"I know you feel awful," I said. I felt bad for my friend, too. But there was also the fate of Four Paws to consider. I cleared my throat. "As hard as this is, I think we need to face some hard facts right now. Tomorrow I plan to visit our remaining clients and the clients we lost. I'll tell them about Charlie—even if they already know—to be transparent. And I'll tell them that their dogs are still safe to walk with us. Because, Lucy, I don't think you should walk the dogs anymore."

I didn't know that I'd been about to say it until I was talking. But this was the only way to move forward. How would the clients trust us otherwise?

Lucy's eyes met mine for the first time, and I could see that hers were red, like she'd been crying.

"Are you firing me?" Lucy asked in a small voice.

"Yes," I said quietly. "I'm sorry."

"That's probably a smart idea," Lucy said, standing up. Before I knew it she was walking out of my room. We both heard the front door of my apartment slam behind her.

"You didn't have to do that," Taz said.

"I'm trying to save the business," I said.

Taz stood up. "I get that. But you might want to think about the price you're willing to pay for it."

Then Taz left, and I was sitting alone. Three half-eaten snack plates sat on my floor, the only sign that my friends had been right here with me, just a few minutes ago.

After sitting frozen for a few more minutes, I made myself get up, clean up the remainders of the snacks, and take them to the trash in the kitchen. Thankfully, Mom and Micki were in their respective rooms, so there was no one around to ask me why I looked so upset. I came back to my room, raced through my homework, and got ready for bed.

But of course I couldn't sleep. I tossed and turned, thinking about the fact that I'd fired Lucy from Four Paws. What did that mean for our friendship? And had I lost Taz's friendship, too? They were my two best friends, and I couldn't imagine life without them. It was almost too much to think about.

I also wondered what exactly I would say to our clients tomorrow to make things better. *If* I could make things better.

20

Borrowing

Lucy was back at school the next day. But in class, she seemed too busy catching up and taking notes to talk to me, and then at lunch she, Brooke, Misty, and Declan went off to practice lines, so Taz and I ate together. We didn't talk about Four Paws at all, but I could feel the tension between us.

At rehearsal, Lucy and I finally interacted. We didn't exactly chat, but she did respond to me when I asked, "Do you know where Mr. Cornell is?"

"I think he went to the restroom," Lucy replied shortly.

"Okay," I said.

And that was that.

Mr. Cornell was clearly relieved to have Lucy back as Emily. She must have practiced her lines on her days off, because she was better than ever.

Unfortunately, *Our Town* is a play that really gives you all the feels, so trying to stay focused on what was best for Four Paws was kind of tough while Lucy gave heartbreaking speeches. Her character *dies*—it's a pretty intense play, really—and comes back as a ghost to visit her family.

As Micki and I listened backstage, Lucy gave her big monologue.

"Goodbye, goodbye, world. Goodbye, Grover's Corners . . . Oh, earth, you're too wonderful for anybody to realize you."

Before I knew it, I felt tears pricking my eyes, and I blinked hard to try to chase them away. Lucy was really killing that scene. I'd wanted to tell her so, but there was so much awkwardness between us. I heard a small *ruff* and looked down at Sparky. Declan's dad had dropped her off again today, and I was glad she was there. I picked her up and cuddled her soft fur to my face.

Then I opened up the side stage door that led outside, being sure to leave it propped open so we could get back in. After she made her business, I sat down in the grass beside Sparky. She ambled up into my lap, and I found myself blinking back tears again. I picked her up again for a much-needed puppy hug.

Oh, how I wanted a dog of my own, instead of having to borrow moments with other people's dogs. Right at that moment, my life felt massively, completely unfair.

Because there was one other thing that this play was forcing me to realize. I was worried that Lucy and Declan seemed to like each other in real life, and it was making me jealous. I hadn't wanted to admit to myself that I was acting differently because of it.

I scooped up Sparky, tried to put on a brave face, and went back in to rehearsal.

I couldn't control the fact that Lucy was mad at me, that she and Declan might have crushes on each other, or that I wasn't allowed to have a dog of my own.

What I could do was save Four Paws.

*   *   *

That evening, as planned, I went knocking on doors all around the Burgundy to talk to our remaining clients about Charlie. I had written an apology speech down in my notebook and knew what to say—that we understood their hesitation, but we wanted a second chance. Still, it was awkward to have to go visit people and tell them you still wanted them to trust you . . . even though one of your dog walkers lost a dog.

It was also harder than I thought it would be to tell people about Lucy being fired.

When I went to try to get Charlotte Willis back as a client, was I imagining her judging look when I told her that I had fired my best friend? Of course, I didn't say it like that. I tried to be professional. And thankfully Charlotte agreed to give us one more chance. And so did Mr. Dana.

But I didn't even try with Mrs. Galanis. I couldn't get past the pit in my stomach when I remembered her tone the day we found Charlie.

A lot of clients weren't home, so eventually I decided to call it a night. There had to be an easier way to reach all of them, I thought as I walked up the stairs back to my floor. Maybe we could send a mass message out on the app, but that felt sort of impersonal.

Sarah was coming back from the laundry room when I arrived on my floor. She waved at me. "Hey, Kat—I know it's later than you usually take him, but would you be willing to walk Meatball?" she asked.

"Of course!" I said, feeling my spirits lift, and I followed her inside.

Meatball came running, as usual. He almost tripped over his own short little legs, he was running so fast. I knelt down and accepted the massive face licking from my favorite furry boy. Then I stood up and got his harness off the hook by the door.

"You have your key?" Sarah asked me, setting down the laundry basket.

"I do. We'll be back in a few," I told her.

It was hard to get Meatball into his harness since he was still wriggling all over the place in excitement.

We only walked for a few minutes before Meatball got down to making his business. I knew I should get him back to the Thompsons, but I spotted a bench, so I picked him up and sat with his warm, furry little body close to me. Just five more minutes, that's all I would borrow. I held on to him with one hand and felt his little heart beating beneath my fingers. I closed my eyes and wished, like I had with Sparky earlier that day, that I could hug him like this whenever I needed. But then I stood up, and Meatball and I headed back home.

As we were walking through the lobby, Marcel stopped me. "Hey, Kat—do you have a second?"

I froze. I'd felt awkward around Marcel ever since he'd been clued in to our Four Paws mishaps. "Sure." I walked over to the tall desk he sometimes sat behind.

"I'm sorry to hear that you're having trouble with your business. Since the whole Charlie incident."

"Thanks, Marcel. I've been trying to get everyone back. I'm just glad we found Charlie and it all worked out okay."

"I think it was really great how you kids organized and found him so fast," he told me. "And I'd like to help you. I asked Mr. Peters about it, and he said you could come and make a presentation at the next Tenants' Association meeting."

"Really?" I said. I'd heard my parents talk about the Tenants'

Association at the Burgundy. At those meetings, a lot of important building decisions got made.

Marcel nodded. "There will be lots of new tenants there this month, since the renovations on the ninth floor are finally complete. It might be a great chance for you to get some new clients, and maybe impress some old ones."

I gripped Meatball's leash tightly. "Oh my goodness, Marcel—that's so great. I don't know what to say, except, thank you!" My mind was already racing about my presentation. I had so many ideas . . .

"You're welcome. I like to see young people working hard instead of just playing video games or wasting time online."

I didn't like public speaking very much, but this was important to Four Paws. "When is the next meeting?" I asked him.

"This Saturday. At seven, in the conference room down here on the main floor."

Not much time to plan . . . was my first thought.

"Okay, great! Thanks again, Marcel!" I waved goodbye, and Meatball and I stepped into the elevator. I pushed the button for my floor, but then I realized something.

Saturday at seven was the exact time of the play at school.

I stood frozen as the elevator started upward. I'd made a commitment to help with the play, even if I wasn't all that great of a stagehand. And how could I miss Lucy's performance, and Declan's? And Brooke's? And Taz had designed all the costumes . . .

But on the other hand, how could I turn down this perfect opportunity to help Four Paws?

As I took Meatball back to Sarah's, my mind bounced back and forth like a rubber ball. First I thought, *I have to be there at the play.* Next I'd realize I just *had* to take the opportunity to present at the Tenants' Association meeting.

Finally, after flip-flopping for hours, I realized what I had to do.

21

Supposed to Be

The chance to make a presentation about Four Paws to all the tenants—especially the new ones—was too good to pass up. I was going to have to miss *Our Town*. Or at least part of it. I figured if I could present first at the meeting, maybe I could make it to the second half of the play after intermission. *Maybe*.

Friday afternoon at rehearsal, I knew I needed to tell everyone that I wouldn't be at the performance the next day. I had already thought about what I would tell Mr. Cornell—that an unforeseen opportunity had come up that I couldn't miss, but I was confident that the other stage crew members (plus Micki, if she wanted to help) would be able to cover for me with no issues. Which I knew was true. But I was still trying to work up the nerve to actually say something.

I looked out onstage. Declan and the other boys in the cast were acting out the scene where George imagines that his baseball team comes in to heckle him on his wedding day.

Declan looked over at me and he smiled.

Somehow that made me feel even guiltier.

The rehearsal went by quickly—too quickly. Lucy was great again (though she still wasn't really speaking to me), and I was sad that Sparky wasn't backstage. Declan's dad had found a non–Four Paws dog sitter for her. Suddenly rehearsal was wrapping up and I still hadn't said anything about missing the actual play. Maybe I would just tell everyone tomorrow that I was sick and couldn't make it?

I felt like a terrible coward. I didn't want to lie. But I just couldn't bring myself to say the words out loud today.

"Come on, Micki!" I called when rehearsal was finished. I felt like my insides were all tied up in knots. I just wanted to get out of there. I noticed that Lucy left the auditorium quickly, without waiting for us.

"I can't find my backpack," Micki told me, looking all around the backstage area.

"Well, where did you leave it?" I asked, feeling my heart race as Declan came backstage.

"Are you walking home?" Declan asked me.

I stared at him for a few seconds, almost blurting out about missing the play but chickening out yet again.

"Are you okay?" he asked when he realized I hadn't said anything.

I shook my head. "No, not really. But yeah, as soon as Mick finds her backpack, we're walking. You, too?" He nodded.

"I've got it!" I heard my sister call, and she skipped over to us, backpack in hand.

Micki, Declan, and I walked home together. Micki chattered away about the play, but I remained silent. Declan kept glancing at me as if he wanted to ask me what was wrong, but I was relieved when he didn't.

When we got back to the Burgundy, Declan's dad met him in the lobby and they headed out for dinner, so Micki and I rode the elevator up alone. Out of habit, I checked the Four Paws app—Taz had taken the walks that night, so we were all set for the day. I knew it wasn't my imagination that the app was quieter than usual.

Micki and I walked inside our apartment to find that Mom wasn't home yet. She had left a note on the fridge board, which said that she'd be home in about an hour but there were sandwiches in the fridge if we were hungry.

Micki got herself a sandwich, but I went back to my room to start working on my presentation for the Tenants' Association. I wished I had some kind of visual aid, but I felt weird about asking Taz to design anything when things with her felt so strained. And Lucy could have easily made me a poster, too, but I knew I couldn't ask. I would just have to use my own skills. I was determined to ace this. Four Paws was all I really had right now. I had to make it work.

I was typing up some speech ideas when I heard Mom come in the front door. She came to stand in my doorway. "Hey, Kat."

"Hey," I said.

"Uh-oh," she began. "Did you already hear the news?"

My head flew up. "What news?"

Mom frowned. "Can I sit?" She gestured toward my bed and I nodded.

"So I was just talking with Sarah Thompson. I ran into her in the elevator. And she shared something with me."

My whole body felt cold. *Are the Thompsons also going to cancel on Four Paws?* "What is it?"

"She told me that they're moving in a few weeks," Mom explained, and I gasped. "To Chicago. It's where Sarah's family is, and she says it's just gotten to the point that she really needs help with the kids. Dan got a job there, and they found a new apartment. I wanted to tell you because I know how attached you are to Meatball."

I tried to swallow past the sudden lump in my throat. "They're leaving?" I repeated. I would have to say goodbye to Meatball? Forever?

"Yes, honey. I'm so sorry."

"Thank you for telling me," I managed to say. It was hard to form the words.

"Sweetie, do you want me to make you some cocoa?" Mom offered.

I shook my head. "No. I'm okay. I just have this thing I have to get ready . . . for school." I hadn't told my mom that I'd be going to the Tenants' Association—and skipping the play—either. I'd tell her tomorrow, I decided. It was too much for tonight.

Mom nodded. "Okay, Kat. But if you want to talk more about this, I'm right here."

I shook my head but then said, "Thanks, Mom."

As I watched her leave, part of me wanted to let her hug me and maybe make me feel a little better. But another part of me was frustrated. If only she'd taken my side with Dad, I'd have my own dog by now, and maybe the idea of losing Meatball wouldn't be making me feel so incredibly sad.

I picked up my phone and hit the button to call Lucy, before I remembered.

I hit the cancel button quickly and wondered if it would register on her phone as a missed call.

I couldn't even talk to my best friend. I'd messed everything up between us, all for the sake of Four Paws. I couldn't call Lucy when I needed her. And I guess that meant she couldn't count on me, either, when she needed *me*.

And that was the moment it hit me. Lucy *did* need me, right now—when she'd messed up with Charlie and was still feeling so badly about it. And she needed me to support her in the play, too.

And I'd failed to be there, because I chose Four Paws instead. I'd been doing exactly what my dad had been doing for the past few years: putting business ahead of the people I loved.

I stared at the words I'd typed on the screen for the presentation, and now it all seemed so meaningless. How could I even think about missing the play? My *best friend's* play?

I stood up and ran out to the kitchen. Mom was making cocoa for herself. "Mom, I have to go see Lucy."

"It's kind of late . . ." Mom began.

"Please?"

"Okay. If it's all right with her mom. And be back in half an hour. Got it?"

I nodded. "Got it."

Not even bothering to wait for the elevator, I started running upstairs.

Out of breath, I knocked on the Larrabees' door.

I didn't know what I was going to say, but all of a sudden, I was completely sure, for the first time in days, that I was standing exactly where I was supposed to be.

22

Every, Every Minute

Ms. Larrabee seemed surprised to see me, but she didn't send me away. She told me I could go knock on Lucy's door. It sounded like maybe she wasn't sure if Lucy would answer. And I wasn't, either.

I stood outside Lucy's bedroom door, my hand poised to knock, feeling sick. How did I get to a place where I was nervous to walk into Lucy's room? Sure, I loved our Four Paws business. But this was *Lucy*. We'd been best friends for years and years.

For weeks, I'd been daydreaming about telling my dad how successful my business had become, when he finally came home.

But then I heard some of the worst news I'd ever heard, and I couldn't even call my best friend to talk about it.

I loved my dad, but now I knew that I didn't want to be like him in every way. Not if it meant losing my best friend.

I knocked. "It's Kat," I said. "Can I come in?"

It took a few seconds, but finally Lucy said, "Okay."

"I'm sorry," I said as soon as I walked in the door.

"What for?" she asked from where she sat on her bed. She still sounded frosty. It made sense. I'd been the one who was cold enough to actually *fire* her.

I took a deep breath. "For putting the business ahead of our friendship," I said.

Lucy looked up at me then, and really looked at me. For the first time in days. "Do you mean that?" she asked.

I nodded. "I do. I . . . I'm not perfect, either. I had no right to get so mad at you. Of course what happened with Charlie was an accident. You would never have lost him on purpose."

"Of course not!" Lucy said, her face flushing.

"So it makes it even worse that I blamed you," I said miserably. I felt tears gathering at the corners of my eyes. "Also, I have a confession to make. I've had my own mishaps with the dogs. I didn't even tell you guys about the time I borrowed the Worthingtons' stroller for Meatball without asking, and Marcel caught me."

"Whoa!" Lucy said, her eyes wide.

I nodded. "And the other day, I was distracted when Micki asked me for a prop backstage, and Sparky got away from me. I can see how fast something like that happens. So I had no right to even judge you at *all*. I don't even know . . . I just . . . I wanted to make the business work . . . *so badly*." I swallowed hard. "You and Taz are *so great* at everything, and I wanted to finally have something I was great at, too."

My voice cracked on that last part, and I really did start to cry. Lucy didn't say anything; she just stood up and came over and hugged me.

"I understand," she said, and it was so much more than I deserved that it made me cry even harder.

"But I was being an idiot," I went on, swiping at my eyes. "Four Paws doesn't make sense without you . . . *I* don't make sense without you. And, Lucy, I've missed you. So much."

Lucy stepped back. "I missed you, too. And I'm sorry, too, Kat. I felt so bad and so embarrassed after losing Charlie... I think I kind of shut you out. I knew how disappointed you were in me."

"I was mostly worried about Charlie. And you. The whole thing was just so terrible."

Lucy nodded. "I know. But I didn't have the chance to tell you—my mom and I had the Porters over for dinner a couple of days ago as a way to try to apologize for what happened with Charlie. They were upset but really understanding. I'm not sure if they'll use Four Paws again, but they said they realize this stuff can happen with any dog sitter. You just have to be careful, and hope for the best."

"It's true," I said. "Dogs chase things. They slip their leashes. Some get lost and never get found. Bad stuff happens. That's life. That's kind of what the play we're doing is about."

Lucy cocked her head to one side. "*We're* doing? Does that mean that you're not going to miss it after all?"

I felt my eyes widen. "How did you . . . ?"

"Marcel asked Taz about that Tenants' Association thing, and she told me."

"You guys both knew?"

She nodded. "We didn't say anything to Declan. I guess we were both kind of hoping that you wouldn't go through with skipping the play."

I shook my head. "I'm not going to. I don't even know what I was thinking. I'm so sorry, Luce. I . . . just heard some bad news, and I went to call you, and then realized you didn't want to talk to me, and then it just hit me. How wrong I've been."

"What was the bad news?" Lucy asked, frowning.

I sighed. "The Thompsons are moving away in a few weeks. I have to say goodbye to Meatball forever."

Lucy gasped and came in for another hug. "I'm sorry, Kat. That's terrible news." I held on to her and appreciated how she always knew exactly what to say. Because she was my best friend.

I pulled away. "Thanks, Luce. But . . . that's not why I'm here. I'm here to try to make things right with you. I just hope I'm not too late . . ."

Lucy started crying then. "Oh, Kat—of course you're not!"

I gave her another hug. "I'm glad. Maybe thanks to *Our Town* I'm finally realizing what's important in life . . . while I live it."

"*Every, every minute,*" Lucy finished the line from the play and swiped at her eyes.

"I *do* still want to make Four Paws a big success," I added. "But there's only one way to do that. Would you consider coming back?"

"I'll consider it," Lucy answered with a smile. "But for now, I have to focus on being awesome onstage. So no business talk until after the play. Deal?"

I smiled back. "Deal."

I hugged my best friend again, then went downstairs, just under the half-hour mark Mom had set. Tomorrow I would think about how hard it would be to explain to Marcel that I had to turn down the great opportunity he'd set up for me. And— much, much harder—how to say goodbye to Meatball.

But for tonight, I had my best friend back. I could face the rest, with her in my corner.

23

Too Wonderful for Anybody to Realize

I woke up on Saturday morning feeling lighter than I had in weeks. Tonight was the play, and I would be there to help, just like I'd promised, and to cheer for my best friend.

I got dressed and went down to the lobby. Telling Marcel that I couldn't do the Tenants' Association presentation after all was hard, but he said he understood, that as I got older I'd find out life was often about making tough choices.

As soon as the play was over, I'd call for a meeting with all four of us Paws, and together we'd come up with another plan.

As for Meatball moving away, I just couldn't even bring myself to think about that. I knew if I did, I'd just start crying and I might not be able to stop.

That afternoon, Micki and I walked to school, both of us in our all-black stage crew outfits. Lucy and Declan and the rest of the cast were getting there a little later, since the stage crew's job was to set up all the props before the actors arrived.

Mr. Cornell looked relieved when he saw us (probably mostly Micki), and I wondered if he'd known—or sensed—that I'd almost missed this event. I was glad I hadn't let him down. The stage crew got busy setting up our props, putting signs for the cast's family members on seats near the front of the auditorium, and running errands for Mr. C.

Before we knew it everything was ready, and the cast was assembled backstage in their costumes. Taz had, of course, done an amazing job with the costumes; she was backstage, too, checking to make sure all the outfits looked good and fixing people's hair. Lucy looked beautiful in her old-fashioned dress with her hair piled up on her head in a bun. And Declan looked so cute in his old-fashioned suit that I thought my heart might have skipped a beat or two when I saw him.

Soon it was showtime. The audience members filed in, and after Mr. C's introduction, I listened to the full hush in the auditorium before the curtains opened.

The play wasn't perfect. I was late with a prop, but Micki saved me. And poor Brooke messed up two of her cues. But by the time Lucy finished her final big monologue, I was sure there weren't many dry eyes in the house. I watched Lucy from the wings, thinking about how we'd made up the night before. My eyes for sure weren't dry at all. I felt a few tears break free as Lucy said the words, *"Oh, earth, you're too wonderful for anybody to realize you."*

Then Misty stepped forward as the Stage Manager and gave the audience the final speech. It went by so fast, and before I knew it, there she was telling the audience, *"Good night,"* the last two words of the play. We'd done it.

The audience burst into loud applause, clapping and cheering.

The cast started walking out onstage to take their bows. I wasn't surprised when Brooke dragged Mr. C out there and handed him a big bouquet of flowers. But I was surprised when some other cast members ran offstage and started bringing stage crew members—plus Taz—onto the stage as well. Lucy and Declan ran offstage, grabbed Micki and me, and brought us onstage with everyone else. Micki and I looked at each other and grinned, then looked out at the audience. The lights onstage were too bright to make out any faces, but from here we could see that people really seemed to have liked the play. They were even all standing up!

Then I glanced down and realized that Declan hadn't let go of my hand after he'd brought me onstage. I felt a small thrill go through me.

We all finished taking our bows, and then we walked off-stage. In the wings, everyone bustled around, hugging each other and moving props and talking about how great everything went. But Declan and I stood still, facing each other, still holding hands. My heart was racing as Declan smiled at me.

"You were fantastic," I told him.

"Thank you," Declan said. "So were you."

I laughed, shaking my head. "I was just behind the scenes."

"But you always make sure everything goes perfectly," Declan said.

"Not perfectly," I said, thinking of the missed prop, of my Four Paws mishaps, of Lucy.

"As long as it's your best, it's perfect." He paused, then said, "You're the best, Kat."

I couldn't catch my breath. Our eyes met. And then . . . Declan leaned in and kissed me.

My first kiss.

Declan stepped back and I blinked as if I were dreaming. The cast and crew were still bustling all around us and hadn't noticed the kiss—but I did catch Micki watching us with a mischievous smile. Her expression seemed to say, *What took you guys so long?*

"I thought . . . I thought you liked . . . someone else," I told Declan, my cheeks burning.

Declan blushed, too. "Are you kidding? Ever since I met you, I've liked *you*, Kat. I thought I was being obvious. But I finally decided to be *more* obvious."

"Well, that . . . works out. Because ever since I met you, I've liked *you*, too." My cheeks burned even redder, but I was glad I'd said it.

Declan squeezed my hand, and together we joined the rest of the cast and crew, who were streaming out of the wings and into the auditorium to find their families and friends. I noticed that lots of cast members were getting big bouquets of flowers.

I was still holding hands with Declan when I spotted Mom, but she was holding hands with someone, too.

Dad was here.

Right away, he noticed me and Declan. "Clearly I've missed some stuff," he said with a smile. Dad handed me a bouquet of flowers, and I let go of Declan's hand to take it.

"I see my dad and brother over there," Declan said, nodding to the other side of the auditorium. "Hi, Mrs. Cabot. Nice to meet you, Mr. Cabot," he added, shaking hands with Dad.

"I'm sure we'll be seeing more of each other very soon," Dad said, giving Declan a look that was maybe a tiny bit stern. Declan shot me a smile before heading off toward his dad and

Aidan. I turned back to my parents, still in a little bit of a daze from the whole experience.

"So anyway, surprise!" Dad said to me. He was holding another bouquet of flowers, and when Micki raced over, he handed the bouquet to her. She squealed and gave him a big hug. Even though I felt a mix of surprise, unease, and happiness at seeing Dad, I gave him a hug, too.

I gestured to my flowers. "You know we weren't actually in the play, right?"

Dad nodded. "I know. Micki told me all about it on our last call. But just because you're not in the cast doesn't mean you haven't both worked hard. I wanted to be here to see you."

"Thanks. That means a lot," I told him, and Dad smiled, ruffling my hair.

Taz hurried over to join us then. I hadn't seen her yet in all the commotion backstage.

"Congrats on the costumes," I told her, and my parents and Micki chimed in with compliments, too.

"Thanks, Cabots," Taz said, her eyes shining. Then she

turned to me. "You did good," she added, and I knew she meant by coming tonight instead of going to the Burgundy meeting.

I gave her a quick hug, and then Taz said she'd catch me later but was going to find Lucy.

Lucy! I looked down at my flowers, realizing that I should have bought some for her.

"Um, Dad? Would you be super mad at me if I gave these to Lucy?"

"No, of course not."

"You can share mine," Micki said quickly, holding up her bouquet.

I flashed her a smile. "Let me just give these to her and then I'll be right back," I said.

I found Lucy surrounded by her mom, her cousins, Taz, and some other kids from our grade. But I pushed through, figuring I had my best friend privileges restored. "Lucy! You were amazing!" I told her, offering her the flowers and giving her a huge hug.

Lucy smiled. "Thanks, Kat! You were, too. I'm so glad you're here!"

"Me too. Listen, my dad is here! So I have to go . . . but we'll text later, okay?"

"Count on it!"

I waved goodbye and went to rejoin my family. "Are you ready?" Mom asked.

"I'm ready," I said. "Who wants pizza?" I asked, giving Micki a wink.

"I do, I do!" Micki yelled, and both our parents laughed. I looked around for Declan as I followed my family outside. I spotted him with his dad and brother, and a lady who had to be his mom. Declan waved at me and I waved back, smiling shyly. My face turned pink as I remembered him kissing me.

The writer of *Our Town* had been right. Sometimes life really was too wonderful for anybody to realize.

24

Seven Paws and Counting

"So how is the business going?" Dad asked me after we got home from dinner.

I took a deep breath. The truth was, our client numbers were still down.

I sat down across from him in the living room. "Not that great, actually. We had kind of a setback."

"The lost dog? Your mom told me about it. But, Kat . . . I do wish that *you* had told me."

I nodded but didn't look up at him. I was playing with the tassel on one of Mom's decorative pillows.

"Kat?" Dad prompted.

"It's hard to talk to you sometimes," I finally managed to say. "When you're away."

"Oh," Dad said after a pause. "I can understand that," he went on. "It's hard for me, too. Especially to hear about things going on in your life and not be around for them."

"I get that," I said.

"Kat, I was glad to see the play you girls worked so hard on. But it's not the real reason I came back." He let out a breath before going on. "Your mom told me about you firing Lucy."

My head flew up. "She did?"

"Yes. She did. Your mom said something to me on the phone, and, Kat, it was like a knife to my gut. She said that she was afraid that you were turning out to be too much like me." Dad's eyes looked kind of bright. I'd only seen him cry a handful of times. It felt strange to see him so upset and to hear him talk so honestly to me. "And that's when I called my boss and said I wanted a demotion."

"What?" I asked, feeling my eyes widen in surprise. "You did?"

Dad nodded. "The amount of travel I've been doing came along with the promotion I got two years ago. So, I asked for my old job back, and she said yes."

"Dad, are you serious?" I couldn't believe what I was hearing. It kind of sounded like Dad had come to the exact same conclusion that I had: deciding to choose the people he loved over his business.

"Totally serious," Dad said. "It's only a small pay cut, and the best thing is, I'll be home a lot more now." Dad looked and sounded relieved.

Once the shock wore off, I launched myself at him and gave him a huge hug.

"Good news?" Dad asked.

I wiped at my eyes. "Yes. These are happy tears. Good news. Very, very good news."

The next couple of weeks were full of good things. Dad was home, and not going on another trip for *six weeks*, which was basically forever—and it was a short one, like he used to take in the old days. Lucy and I were best friends again, and Taz wasn't mad at me anymore, either. And Declan and I were, well, I supposed we were boyfriend and girlfriend now. Although we hadn't said the words out loud, we held hands in the hallway, sat together every day at lunch, sometimes walked Sparky together after school, and texted in the evenings until one of our parents took our phones away. Taz and Lucy were totally supportive of the relationship—Lucy wasn't even remotely jealous, only excited for me. And Taz said, "Just don't start kissing in front of us at any Four Paws meetings."

Even without my presentation at the Tenants' Association meeting, Four Paws business seemed to be doing pretty well again. Now that the play was over, Taz had time to create new flyers, so we'd even gotten some new clients.

The only bad thing in all the good? Meatball was leaving New York in a matter of days. With the family getting ready for the move, I'd been taking Meatball on almost all his walks. I tried not to count down in my head to the final time, but I kept doing it anyway. One day, we just sat in the park on a bench while I cried on his fur. Two different strangers had stopped to ask me what was wrong.

So that night, when both Mom and Dad were at dinner, I brought up my greatest wish one more time.

"Mom, Dad," I said, and they both looked surprised that I sounded so serious. "Four Paws has gotten some clients back. And I have continued to take great care of everyone's dogs."

"You don't have to tell us all of that, Kat," Mom said. "We know you're a responsible kid."

"And we're so proud of you for pursuing something you're passionate about," Dad added.

"Thanks," I said. "So . . . can we get a dog for Christmas?"

Mom and Dad looked at each other with guarded expressions. "It's a possibility," Dad said.

"That's not a yes," Micki grumbled.

"It's not a no, either," Mom pointed out.

I'd told myself I wouldn't pull this guilt card, but it spilled out of me. "It's just, with Meatball leaving . . . it's hard to imagine loving another dog as much as him, but I know I would love our dog with all my heart."

"Oh, Kat," Mom said, placing her hand on mine. "I know you're sad about Meatball. We'll see, okay? We'll see."

*   *   *

On Saturday, Meatball's next-to-last day, Declan and I were hanging out in his living room, playing with Sparky. His dad was in the spare room he used as his studio, and his music traveled down the hall.

Declan rolled his eyes. "Angsty nineties rock. The sound track to my life, whether I want to hear it or not."

I giggled and scratched Sparky's pale little belly. She let out a happy bark. She was getting so big now—hardly a puppy anymore.

"So it sounds like you might get your own dog for Christmas," Declan said. I'd filled him in on my conversation with my parents, of course.

"I hope so. My parents haven't officially said yes yet. But they seem more open to the idea than before."

"Fingers crossed," Declan said. "I'm sure Sparky would love to have a doggie friend she could play with all the time."

I smiled, thinking a little sadly about how well Sparky and Meatball got along.

My phone buzzed in my pocket and I pulled it out. My mom had texted our emergency family code: the word *now* in all caps with four exclamation points.

I jumped up. "I have to go. When my mom texts this, it's some kind of emergency. Man, I hope it's nothing bad! Mostly everything's been going so amazing lately."

"Mostly?" Declan asked, pulling me in for a hug.

"You know very well you're in the *going-amazing* category, Declan Ward."

"Yeah, I know," he said. He pulled me closer again and gave me a quick kiss. "Text me an update. Okay?"

"Okay," I said. "Bye, Sparky!"

She gave a short bark, and I headed out the door. When I got back to my apartment, I knocked and thought I heard barking, but it must have been my imagination.

Mom answered the door. "You forget your key?"

I nodded. "Yeah, sorry."

"Well, come on in. Your dad and I have something to show you."

"Where's Micki?" I asked.

"She's at her friend Grace's, remember? Besides, we wanted to talk to you first about this."

"Okay . . ." I said, feeling a little nervous. Why was Mom being so weird?

"There's been a change of plans," Dad said when I walked into the living room. "We *were* planning to get a puppy for you in December."

Oh no. I'd jinxed myself just a few minutes ago, talking to Declan. Now my parents were about to tell me that the getting-a-dog deal was off. I'd been foolish to hope.

"What happened?" I asked.

"Well, another dog became . . . available," Dad said.

My ears perked up at that. I *thought* I'd heard barking. Was my new dog here, now?

"What do you mean, 'available'?" I asked, my heart pounding.

"Well, we knew you wanted a black pug. And it turns out, they aren't all that common," Mom said. "I don't know if you realize that. But actually, this dog isn't a puppy at all. And we spoke to his owners, and it seems they're moving and can't bring the dog to their new home . . ."

I felt a kernel of hope bloom in my chest. Could it be possible that my parents were talking about . . . my Meatball?

"Do you mean . . . ?" I asked, my voice coming out breathless.

Mom nodded. She looked over at Dad. "Yes. Sarah Thompson came to visit the other day. She and Dan were talking about the move and how stressed the family has been. She was really worried about taking Meatball in the car the whole way, and isn't sure they can really handle acclimating him to a new place, and . . . anyway, they think it's best for Meatball if they don't move him to Chicago."

"Oh my gosh," I whispered.

Mom beamed at me. "Sarah told us that no one cares for or loves Meatball like you do. She said she knew it was a long shot, but before she tried to re-home him somewhere else she wanted to at least ask us."

I stood frozen in shock, barely daring to believe it. But then Dad walked back toward my room and emerged leading

Meatball on his leash. Dad had to let go when my boy caught sight of me. Meatball barreled toward me, and I launched onto the floor and scooped him up into my arms. I kissed his ears and the sides of his face and got tons of sloppy tongue kisses in return. I was laughing and crying all at the same time.

"I guess she's excited," Dad said to Mom.

"I guess so," Mom said.

I looked up at my parents and grinned. "Thank you," I said. "Oh, thank you! I'll take such good care of him."

"We know you will. You *and* Micki will," Dad added with a laugh.

Mom and Dad left me alone with my new dog for a few minutes. I gazed into his deep brown eyes and couldn't believe he was really going to be my dog forever.

I thought of another line from *Our Town*, about how the stars make their crisscross journeys around the sky. Life was like that, too, I guessed. Dad was back mostly to stay, but now the Thompsons were leaving. Declan had come to the Burgundy, and now I couldn't imagine life without him. Lucy, Taz, and I were best friends again, and Meatball, whom I thought I'd lost for good, well, he was home to stay. Forever.

Now I had *seven* wonderful Paws in my life, I thought as I cuddled Meatball close. Lucy, Taz, Declan, and all four adorable paws on my little Meatball.

And who knew? Maybe Micki would join Four Paws once she was a little older. It would be a lot of fun, sharing Meatball with her. And Brooke, whom I'd talked to the other day at school, had mentioned that she'd be spending more time with her mom who lived in the neighborhood. So she might become a part-time Paw, too. The business was growing.

I'd been so anxious about trying to make the business a success, but now I wasn't nervous anymore: Whatever happened with Four Paws, I knew it would all turn out okay. After all, that's the real secret to a great business, if you ask me. Great friends.

Meatball gave me another sloppy kiss and I giggled.

Well, great friends . . . *and* adorable dogs.

Acknowledgments

Girls just wanna have pugs . . . and fun . . . and thanks to Aimee Friedman and Olivia Valcarce, my writing life has been paws-itively full of both! Here's to another furry adventure hitting the shelves.

Thank you to my agent, Devin Ross, for always being in my corner—next time we're getting cookies!

As always, thanks, Mom, for our daily chat, and a special shout-out to my family in PA: Jim, Laura, Grace, Matthew, and welcome to baby Henry.

Thank you to my Palm Beach Day Academy family. I love spending my days with all of you.

Finally, thank you to every reader who's spent time with Potato, Osito, Pancake, Pepper, Jack, Cupid, and now Meatball. You guys are TOTALLY PAWSOME!

Don't miss these other pug-dorable reads by J.J. Howard!

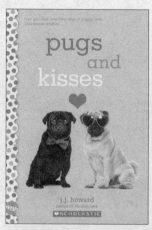

Read the latest (wish) books!

shake it off

pumpkin spice up your life

Natalie Blitt

Snow One Like You

TWICE UPON A TIME

Robin Hood

WANTED

The One Who Looked Good in Green

WENDY MASS
New York Times bestselling author of 11 Birthdays

the love pug

J.J. Howard
Author of Pugs and Kisses

pugs in a blanket

J.J. Howard
Author of Pugs and Kisses

girls just wanna have pugs

J.J. Howard
Author of Pugs and Kisses

ANGELA CERVANTES

LETY OUT LOUD

alpaca my bags

Jenny Goebel

YAMILE SAIED MÉNDEZ

Random Acts of Kittens

Can she find three kittens their forever homes?

meow or never

It's never too late to make a new friend.

SCHOLASTIC

scholastic.com/wish

WISHSPRING21